THE BLUE

Maggie Gee

THE BLUE

TELEGRAM
London San Francisco Beirut

British Library Cataloguing-in-Publication Data
A catalogue record for this book is available from the British Library

ISBN 10: 1-84659-013-2
ISBN 13: 978-1-84659-013-9

This edition published 2006 by Telegram Books

Manufactured in Lebanon

TELEGRAM
26 Westbourne Grove, London W2 5RH
825 Page Street, Suite 203, Berkeley, California 94710
Tabet Building, Mneimneh Street, Hamra, Beirut
www.telegrambooks.com

This collection is dedicated to my beloved editor and friend,
Christine Casley, 1933–2005:

into the blue

Acknowledgments

'The Blue': A first draft of this story was written for a British Council visit to Libya in 2002. It was first published in *Tell Tales 2,* edited by Rajeev Balasubramanyam (Flipped Eye Publishing, 2005).

'The Artist' was first published in *Diaspora London* (Arcadia Books, 2003).

'Thank You Tracey Emin' was first published in *YOU* magazine, *The Mail on Sunday*, 2001.

'Righteousness' was broadcast by BBC Radio 3's *The Verb* in 2006.

'The Good Hope' was read at Cheltenham Festival and on BBC Radio 4, and first published in *The New Statesman*, 2002.

'Good People' was written for Courttia Newland and Nii Parkes's *Tell Tales 1* tour, 2004.

'The Money' was commissioned by Cheltenham Festival in 2003. It was broadcast on BBC Radio 4 and first published in Ian Irvine's *Talk of the Town* supplement of *The Independent on Sunday*.

'Starting at Last' was first published online by www.pulp.net, 2004

'Mornington Place' was first published in *London Tales*, edited by Julian Evans (Hamish Hamilton, 1983).

'Beautiful Things' was first published in *The Daily Telegraph*, 1994, and included in *The Daily Telegraph Book of Contemporary Short Stories*, edited by John Coldstream (Headline Review, 1995).

Contents

The Blue

The woman had lived through the longest day, which was boiling hot, in the city, pressing and sieving her into tiny pieces. She had five children; they all needed something, though the elder ones were at university.

'Mum!'

'Mum!'

'Mum!'

'Mum!'

'MU-U-M!!'

'Sorry,' she said, 'Sorry.'

She worked in a dry cleaner's, cleaning other people's clothes. That day, two of the machines had broken down. She had lost three ties and an expensive jacket. A woman came in and said she was a thief. A man had called her an idiot.

'Sorry,' she said. 'Sorry, sir.'

The air was dry and chemical. She wished she could wash the clothes in the river. She and her mother used to do that together.

At three, the woman cleared up to go home. Cleaning other people's clothes made her dirty; she itched from the solvents; she smelled of sweat. She pulled a white hair from her dark cotton shirt. Now she must go home and cook for her husband.

The traffic was a solid wall of metal. In her own metal box it got hotter and hotter. She hung one arm outside the open window. Then she saw a man in the car alongside, making obscene gestures and grinning at her. She drew in her arm and closed the window, but she heard him yell 'Bloody women drivers!'

'Sorry,' she muttered, feeling small and frightened.

But then something inside her began to expand. Something like a distant pool of blue water. She heard the traffic horns, the revving engines, the man who thought she was a bloody woman, but inside her head there was a great pool of quiet. She drove off the road and left her car.

She began to walk down the familiar track. All her life she had been too busy, she hadn't come here since she was a girl, but her feet remembered the way to go.

A beggar sat by a baking wall. 'Give me money, rich woman,' he said, reproachfully.

The woman had worked all day for almost nothing.

'No,' she said. 'No, sorry.'

She kept on walking; he shouted after her. A cloud of blue butterflies drifted towards her across the dry fields, and danced alongside her, so she could no longer see his small cross shape.

A little further on, by a ruined temple, a gang of teenagers were howling with laughter. They had painted slogans on the walls.

'Have you got the time, old woman?' they shouted. 'Tell us the time!' They pulled at her wrist. They didn't want the time, they wanted to hurt her.

'No,' she said. 'No, sorry.' A butterfly was spread where her watch had once been.

Now the track led on past the elaborate back gardens of the large new houses that faced the sea. People had erected gates and fences where she had once wandered with a troupe of goats. A uniformed man with a revolver suddenly stepped out from behind a hedge.

'What are you doing here?' he asked. His dark glasses bored into the hole in her sleeve, scraped up and down the dust on her legs. 'We don't want beggars here, woman. Get back where you belong, pauper.'

'No,' she said, 'No, sorry,' and the cloud of butterflies bobbed up around his head, making him shudder and flap his arms, while she slipped past him, on down the path.

A tiny snicket led off to the right past a sweet-scented patch of *reseda* blossoms. She remembered, with a pang, her mother's grave. Her mother lay waiting in the little cemetery, pleading for something that life had not given her. Her thirsty voice whispered 'Please, daughter.' But how could she make things right for her mother? How could she ever bring enough flowers? The cemetery lay in the wrong direction. 'No,' she said. 'Sorry, dear one.' She picked a tiny spire of sweet *reseda*, and the hot wind carried it towards her mother.

The last part of the track was beyond the arch of the new white university. She was proud that her elder children went there. An ancient scholar sat bowed to the ground, reading a heavy tome, in the shade of the arch. He wrinkled up his eyes at her, over gold glasses.

'Where are you going, young woman?' he asked. 'This place is only for those who love learning.'

'My children love learning,' the woman replied.

'Where are your books?' he insisted, sharply. 'None of the unlearned come through here. Go back home and study, young woman.'

'No,' she said. 'No, sorry,' and two of the butterflies flew from her shoulders and landed, one each, on his spectacle lenses, so he could no longer peer at her.

In the distance, under a spreading tree, her elder children were debating with others. Usually they only saw her in the kitchen. They spotted her just as she was leaving the campus and heading on down towards the wide white sand.

'Mum,' they called, astonished. 'Mum! MU-UM! Where are you going?'

Her heart tugged and pulled, but the core of her was deep blue certainty, an ocean of water.

'Nowhere,' she whispered. 'Sorry, children,' and the butterflies swarmed into a flickering, glistening veil of blue air that hid her from sight. She was alone; all the voices faded.

She padded across the blazing sand. Glad, glad: everything was glad. She knew she could only bear it for a few seconds, but a few seconds would be enough. She took off her clothes. In the distance, people shouted. But the butterflies covered every inch of her body, floating up like blue steam as she slipped into the water. Cool, edgeless, it became her skin. A blue cloud hung on the blue sea wind. She was invisible. She was her soul. Mysterious, liquid, endless, whole.

The Artist

When Boris had only been with her a month, he came in from the garden holding a rose, a dark red complicated knot of velvet. Bowing slightly, he placed it in her fingers. 'Broke in accident', he explained (he was repointing the brick at the back). It was her own rose he was offering her with that graceful, cavalier flourish. 'Put in water, Emma, please.'

'Beautiful, Boris,' she said, inhaling deeply, once, then again. The scent of the rose was so intense it shocked her, made her throat catch and her eyes prickle, as if life was suddenly all around her, as if she was breathing for the first time in years. Emma had hay fever, and avoided flowers. 'So beautiful, I shall write about it.' (She wrote novels, which had never been published, but she had a study, and told people she wrote.)

'I am artist', said Boris, grinning at her with self-deprecating, dark-eyed charm. His teeth were very white, but one was chipped; he had a handsome, cherubic face. 'I am artist, you see, Emma. I am artist like you.' He jabbed his brown finger towards her, laughing. 'I make beautiful house for you.'

'Wonderful, Boris. Thank you. But really I just need the tiles laying out in squares. One black, one white, and so on.'

'Emma, I like you very much. I make you a beautiful floor, it is my present to you.' He bowed extravagantly, a knight. How old was he? Forty, fifty? 'I am artist, Emma,' he continued, showing her a piece of paper on which he had sketched an elaborate black and white design. 'You don't want one square – two square – one square – two square, black, white, same thing always. Very boring. No good!'

She took the paper from him, folded it narrowly, and slipped it back into the pocket of his jacket. 'That's just what I do want. Black, white, black, white. Like a chessboard. Simple. The tiles are in the garage. Now, I must go and work.'

Boris smiled at her forgivingly. 'Yes, you do your work, Emma, you write your books, beautiful. I like this very much, to work for an artist, like me.'

The rose was lovely, though slightly battered. She kissed it lightly before throwing it away.

'He's impossible,' she complained lazily to her husband as they lay in bed with their books, looking at Edward over her glasses, his familiar pinched profile in the cool blue room. She wanted to tell him, she wanted to tell someone, that Boris had given her a rose. 'Impossible. Edward? I'm talking to you.'

'Who is? For heaven's sake, I'm reading my book.'

'Boris,' she said.

He sat up and stared. 'Why do you keep talking about *this person*? Get a proper builder, an English one.'

'I tried, if you remember. You said the price was outrageous.

When you heard Boris's quote, you were very happy.'

'You found him, not me.'

'You agreed we should ask him.'

Edward couldn't deny it. He changed tack. 'You can't manage tradesmen, you never could. The cleaners never do what you tell them to.'

'The cleaners always leave. Because you won't let me pay them enough.'

'I'll talk to the fellow. I'll sort him out.'

'– No, Edward. It's fine, really.' She knew how Edward would talk to Boris. He would send him away, as he had threatened to do. Then the house would be empty every day. She liked Boris's voice, and his accent, which spoke to her of strange wide spaces somewhere far away in southeast Europe, hot stony fields, bright market-places, somewhere she would never go, she supposed, since now she so rarely went out at all. She could never tell Edward about the rose. Her memory of it wilted, faded. 'It's okay, Edward. Boris is – different.'

'What the hell does that mean?' How scornfully he spoke. Had he always spoken to her like that?

'Boris feels he's an artist. He isn't, of course. But he wants to be.' She enjoyed this thought. Poor Boris. What Emma did, he only dreamed of.

'Fraud and con man, like all the others. I want him out by the end of the week. Now could I *please* get on with my book?'

But she saw he was reading his Antiques Almanac, which surely could not have much of a plot-line. 'He lost everything, you know. In that bloody awful war. He didn't choose to come here. But now we can help him.' Saying it, Emma was suffused with love.

17

Edward sighed with irritation. 'He's just an illegal. That's why you're using him. Because he's cheap.' He snapped his book shut, lay down abruptly, and presented her with his navy silk back, taking off his glasses, clicking down the arms. 'A guy in the office said Afghans are cheaper. Good night, Emma.' In minutes he was snoring.

In September, when he should have been clearing out the drains, Boris had brought round his wife and daughter in a rusty, dust-covered grey saloon.

'Van break down. Very sorry.'

'Never mind, come in and get started.'

'No can do. I am in car, with wife, daughter ... I can come in for cup of coffee, Emma, only.'

Boris loved her real coffee, which reminded him of home. 'Actually, I'm writing,' she protested, but he had already barrelled past her, sighing.

'What about your wife, your daughter?'

'They are well, thank you, Emma. Except only daughter –'

'I mean, you can't leave them out in the car, Boris.' It was a bore, but good manners demanded it.

'Yes, they love it.'

'Of course they don't love it. Go and ask them in.'

They trooped up the path, very straight-faced, in front of Boris, who drove them before him like sheep, looking off contemptuously to one side with a smile that seemed to say to the neighbours, 'I know, but these were all I could get.' 'Wife,' he jabbed one finger towards a thickset, grey-faced woman with hostile, uncomprehending eyes. 'Daughter,' and he put his hand on the girl's shoulder, but this time his voice was tinged with love and regret. 'Anna,' he added. 'Seventeen'. She was pretty, with her father's white teeth and cherub nose, but her skin and lips were pale, too pale, her eyes had a slightly sunken look, and she was leaning on her mother.

'Hallo Anna,' Emma smiled at the daughter. To the wife she tried 'I'm sorry, I don't know your name', but the woman's reply meant nothing to her. The words were guttural, unfamiliar.

'Will they have tea or coffee?' she asked Boris.

'No, they don't like,' said Boris, pushing them into the drawing-room, while trying to shepherd Emma back into the dining-room where the serious business of coffee would go on. 'Maybe daughter will have water.'

'Lemonade? Biscuits?'

'They don't want.'

'Water? I can hardly give them just *water*.'

Emma had broken away from Boris, doing her duty, reluctantly, and followed the two women into the drawing-room, where she found them standing together in front of the fireplace. 'Sit down,' Emma said, and they did, too promptly. 'Cake? Fruit juice? Milk? Herbal tea?'

The daughter took pity on her and explained. 'My mother speaks nothing,' she said. 'We like water, thank you, only water.'

'Water, okay then,' Emma said, reluctantly.

She got two glasses, but forgot to fill them, dreaming while Boris's coffee brewed. In the dining-room, Boris was inspecting, with what was surely self-conscious over-emphasis, the prints on the walls, frowning upwards, pursing his lips, nodding judiciously.

'Yes, very beautiful,' he said aloud, looking, not by accident, she thought, at a Lucian Freud of a naked woman. He must want her to see that he liked bare flesh. Such a terrible flirt! Though of course, she was flattered ... He made as if to notice her a few seconds later. 'Daughter is ill,' he hissed.

'Oh dear, Boris.'

'Yes, I take to the doctor. But she need clean air. Air here very dirty. She cannot breathe, Emma. London very bad. Is dust, where we live, damp also. No good.'

'Oh, has she got asthma? What a shame –'

'Asthma, yes. In my country, she hasn't got it. Now she pray every day to Virgin, but she get it very bad.'

'I am so sorry, Boris. But don't worry. I myself have atrocious hay fever. They're all allergies. Have you considered acupuncture?' She mimed little needles jabbing into her arm. 'Maybe aromatherapy?'

He shook his heavy, curly head mournfully. 'Injection? No. Too much – never mind. More coffee, please, Emma.'

Invited in, at first, on a strictly limited basis, to repoint the fireplace, then repaint the drawing-room, Boris's role slowly became a roving one, as different parts of the house demanded his attention. He would announce these impending tasks to Emma, with a mixture of sorrow and glee.

Their relationship progressed in fits and starts. Boris nearly always complimented her. She had striking blue eyes, she had always known that, but he noticed the effect of different colours that she wore, and one day told her he would like to paint her.

'First paint my house,' she said, fondly, and he looked at her with a strange regret that made her think he was a little in love. It wasn't so surprising; she was still quite pretty, and his benefactor, and a writer. But her books became a stumbling block. Boris took everything literally; she had told him she wrote books, when he first came to the house. After a few months he asked if he could see one, just to flatter her, she thought, of course, and she deflected it. But he kept on asking, becoming more pressing, and in the end she had been forced to explain: she hadn't actually published any books. He seemed unreasonably disappointed. Was there a slight dimming of his admiration?

Boris was doing the exterior paintwork when Edward put his foot down. 'When will this clown get the job finished?' he raged at his wife.

'It's been very wet.'

'It isn't now. Has he been here today?'

'His daughter's been ill this week, so he's hardly been in,' Emma said, placatingly, but Edward glared at Boris's paint-pots straggling across the patio, and his brushes in tins of cloudy white spirit, sticking up at the sky at an irritating angle.

'He's never going to darken my doors again if he doesn't get the bloody job done and this mess out of the way before Friday!' he exploded. 'I mean it, Emma. Don't think I don't. We'll get in a decent English builder at last.'

Next day Boris arrived around four, looking worried. After giving up for months, he smelled of smoke again. 'Anna is in the hospital,' he explained. 'I just come to tell you how she is, Emma.'

She didn't make him tea. 'Edward says you have to finish the job by Friday or never come back, and he means it,' she said.

'She is very bad, Emma. Tea with sugar, please.'

'No, he is *serious*,' she said. 'You have to get it done.'

But Boris suddenly clutched her fingers, with an odd little moan. 'Last night they make us stay with her in hospital. Daughter's face goes blue ...'

She pulled her hand away. 'Boris what are you going to do?' she yelled at him, feeling her power at last, losing her temper with his handsome tanned face, his white broken teeth, his thick stupid curls, his foreign problems, the swamp of his need, sucking down tea and coffee and kindness, the scruples that stopped him making love to her, his pallid, boneless daughter and grey hopeless wife, the way he'd made her husband cross with her.

He looked shocked. 'Not to shout, Emma. I am sensitive, like you. I am artist. Not to shout.' He looked as though he was going to cry.

'All right, Boris. But you must get the job done.'

He rang on the door at seven thirty next morning, half an hour earlier than ever before. Emma was bleary and vague, in a hastily donned jade silk kimono. Boris's eyes ran automatically over her body, but his mouth was a line, and his eyes were bloodshot. 'Daughter very sick last night,' he said. 'Van is no good again. And I haven't car, because wife must have it to visit hospital. Emma, you will drive me.'

'Drive you where?'

'Drive me to find men.'

22

'Why haven't you found them already?' She screamed at him.

Boris was frightened of this new savage woman, so different from the mild, flirtatious one he knew. 'Please, Emma. I know where we find men. But quick, drive me now, please.'

'I'm not dressed,' she said. Not that she often did get completely dressed, nowadays, for why go out? Most days Boris came in. 'Emma, put on clothes now,' he insisted. She liked him sounding masterful, and went off upstairs without protesting, returning dressed in the first thing she found in her cupboard, a smart Chanel-copy suit with gold buttons and pink braid.

He looked at her strangely as she came downstairs, but he bowed slightly, and she felt exalted. She was excited: it was an outing. She didn't listen to what he was saying.

'Slow down,' he said, in the northern suburbs. 'Here we find men, Emma.' His mobile rang and he swore and dived for it. As the traffic waited at a bottleneck, he listened intently, then shouted at the phone, finally clicking it off after an explosion of furious consonants. Emma was surprised to see tears in his eyes.

'Are you all right, Boris?' she asked him, tentative.

'Yes, Emma. Now I do work.'

'But you're crying, Boris.'

'Is only dust.'

'Oh. That's good.'

Her attention was distracted. She was driving down a long desolate road, straight, running between Victorian terraces, but there was something in front of the terraces, something that at first she mistook for trees, grey shapeless trees with aimless branches, one or two hundred metres of trees, something that struck her as strange in a city, but then she realised they were not trees. They were thickets of men, standing in clumps, mostly silent, staring at the traffic, men in rough clothes with worn brown skin, men looking furtive, men looking hungry, men with no colour beneath their tans. Dozens of them. Scores. Hundreds? Not a single woman among those thin faces. Washed out tracksuits, ill-fitting trousers. Some of their hair was white with dust. Most of them were smoking lethargically. The slogans on their chests looked tired, dated.

'What is it, Boris? What's going on?'

'Here we find men. Stop car. I do it.'

'I don't want these people!' she found herself shouting. They looked ill and strange, not exotic like Boris. Scenting interest, some had turned towards the car. They were calling out, but she couldn't understand them. Then she caught some broken English: 'Only fifty!' 'Only forty!' She felt naked and stupid in her pink Chanel ribbons and terrible glittering golden buttons.

'Not to shout, Emma.' He looked very weary. 'Is okay. You leave to me.'

'They're not coming in my house. I want proper workmen.'

'Is workmen, Emma.' His phone rang again. He cursed, and threw it down on the back seat, got out of the car and left her alone.

On the pavement, Boris started talking to people. She sat inside trembling, clutching the steering-wheel. What if they suddenly rushed the car, snatched her handbag, raped her, mugged her? The phone rang again, urgent, painful. After thirteen rings she picked it up. A woman's voice shouted in an unknown language. 'I don't understand,' Emma whispered. The woman's cries became more desperate. 'I don't understand. Speak English, please,' Emma said. 'You're in England now. Please speak English.'

She felt better as she said it, briefly, in this unfamiliar place, that had no rules; she stood up for something she thought she believed in, but then the phone went silent, dead, and she laid it on the seat, and felt worse than ever. It must have been his wife. She spoke no English.

Boris came back with three hangdog giants. They got into the back without speaking a word. There was a smell of metal, and old cigarette smoke. They would make her car smell of men – for Edward was not, in that sense, a man.

'I think your wife phoned,' she said to Boris.

He shrugged. He would not look at her. 'Drive home please Emma. We finish the painting.'

The cloud had cleared by the time they got back, and the sun drilled through, fiercely hot. That long dark road with its unhealthy armies had left her with a spreading weight of terror. Boris had come to her on false pretences; he had let her imagine him framed by blue mountains, aromatic meadows, sturdy flocks, but now she saw he just came from this, a sour sad place where no one was happy.

They worked all day, the three strangers and Boris. She heard him shout at them from time to time. She went out twice, nervously, to see what they were doing, and offer tea, but Boris refused, waving one hand in dismissal, going on painting with the other one. She felt unsettled, sitting bowed in her study, trying to invent a love story, safe in her room in the cool pleasant house but uneasily aware of the four male bodies crawling all over it, obsessed, intent, locked to her hot surfaces, sweating, grunting.

The men stayed till seven, and then filed in, burnt red by the sun, hair splashed with white, lips grey-coated, refusing to look her in the eyes. They seemed barely human. She went out and inspected. The job was finished. Boris spoke to the others, who looked only at him, as if Emma herself hardly existed.

She needed Boris to smile at her. 'Would you like a drink, Boris?' she pleaded. 'You must be thirsty after all that work. While I put the money in an envelope.'

'No thank you, Emma. Men wait outside.'

'Oh, they'll be all right. They'll be perfectly happy.'

'No thank you, Emma. I go now, please.'

When Edward arrived, they had just disappeared. He was itching for a fight: the train was hellish, boiling. 'Did he bloody well turn up?' he shouted in the hallway.

'Go out and have a look', said her voice from the study.

Five minutes later, Edward came back in and appeared at her door, actually smiling. 'At long last,' he said. 'Doesn't look too bad. And he's finally cleared all his paint pots away. The whole bloody lot. Why are you crying?'

In November, some tiles blew off the roof, and Edward instructed her to telephone Boris. She had missed him, sharply, day by day. When she tried his number, it was unobtainable. She rang it repeatedly, swearing and weeping.

Next day she got dressed as soon as Edward was gone and drove to the suburbs, remembering. Boris's sweet dark eyes, the slight roughness of his jaw. He had opened doors for her. Surely he liked her. He gave her a rose. He ... admired her.

The forest of men was there, as before. She kept nearly stopping, was afraid, drove on, and finally drew up beside a young, slight man. He had a thin clever face, and black eyes like Boris's. Perhaps he came from the same country. She thought his mouth was quite appealing.

At twelve o'clock she called him in for coffee. 'Thirsty on the roof,' she said, kindly, with elaborate mime to help things along. 'I understand you,' he said, 'It's okay. Nearly everything, I understand. In my own country, I learned good English. I am a student. I *was* a student –' (Yes, she thought, they are all students. The minicab drivers all claimed to be students.) '... sixteenth and seventeenth century history ... I am here because of the war.' He started to talk about invasions, displacements. Oh dear, she thought, he may be a bore.

'Where are you from?' she cut in. He told her.

'My last man came from there,' she said. She felt a rush of hope and pleasure. She told him the name. 'Perhaps you know him. Very hard workers, your countrymen.'

His face had changed. It was charged with interest. 'But Boris is a great man,' he said.

'Excellent worker,' she agreed.

'Is a great artist,' he said.

She laughed. It was charming, how they all praised each other. Every single one was a genius.

'No, really,' he said, 'He is an artist. We think he is a genius.'

27

'Yes, Boris liked to think he was an artist. That's why we got on. I am artistic, too.'

'In my country, Boris is a very great artist. Abroad you don't know him, but in my country ... But now I think he says he will do no more painting.'

She wasn't sure she had understood him. For a moment she'd thought he meant actual art. 'Yes, he's stopped working for me, since the summer,' she said. 'That's why we need a new man, really.'

She went to the kitchen to fetch some biscuits. He carried on talking in the rich, empty room. 'Boris says he will do no more painting. Is a great loss for my country. He says life is over, since his daughter died. His beautiful daughter died, in August.'

The packet wouldn't open; she was wrenching it, noisily, crashing bourbon biscuits on to bone china, but she managed to pick out the single word 'daughter', and remembered Boris's wife, her misery, the apples she ate, her grey distance. The wife and daughter had spoiled it all. 'Are you married?' she called back through from the kitchen.

He shook his head. 'Life is too hard to marry,' he said. 'Life is beautiful, but life is short.'

'I see you are sensitive,' she said, 'like me. I am an artist, you know. I write. There will be other jobs for you,' she said, smiling.

Thank You Tracey Emin

It began that freezing spring.

Joe walked down the riverbank on his own, looking at the huge glass TATE sign catching the sunlight, silver-blue-green in the sun. Just the thought of it made him feel young. If only Amber had come ... Did she still love him? Did she even like him?

(They had met as art students, marched for peace and against the National Front together, missed several marches because they were in bed, honeymooned in Portugal, then, grown more daring, seen life's golden ribbon spool away into the future as they roared down the coastal roads of Australia, backpackers, surfers, a lifetime ago. They had worked on sheep farms and blinked, overwhelmed, at the great blinding deserts of the southwest. 'I'm glad we've seen it, Joe. Now we can go home,' she had said to him, urgently, dwarfed by the light. And they headed home, and she'd become a teacher. Seeing her talent, Joe had once said 'You be the artist, darling, I'll keep you, I could make a fortune in computers.' But neither of them, somehow, had quite made it.)

Tate Modern was chilly and bright inside, like a glamorous

station concourse. There was a series of 'London' rooms showing films. The one he liked best was about Tracey Emin, who was famous. She hovered above him on the wall with her mate Sarah Lucas, two enormous celluloid Madonnas, glowing and giggling and drinking red wine. Tracey Emin was brown and merry like a gipsy, and her face was lopsided when she smoked and laughed, and her voice wasn't bossy like her friend's. And he liked her name. 'Tracey Emin,' he said to himself, like a mantra.

There was a wonderful golden openness about the girls' stunt which made him smile as he walked away across Blackfriars Bridge. Though he had to admit that the British section was a bit thin compared to the other countries, who seemed to have put a bit of effort in. As he walked, he began to feel sorry for all the young artists who weren't Tracey Emin or Sarah Lucas or Damien Hirst. There might be some who could actually do things like paint or sculpt or whatever ... but how could they ever get famous while this gang of charming tossers burned up all the oxygen?

Joe had a sudden bolt of lightning.

He, himself, had a space.

He had an office so dull that it sent him to sleep. Joe thought, I am going to turn my office into a gallery, so I can work surrounded by beauty. Young artists will like me. My life will change.

He smiled at the bright blue wind from the river, and thought 'Thank you, Tracey Emin.'

One Saturday, six months later, Joe and Amber were walking towards his office in Harlesden.

They both saw it at the same moment.

A suitcase stood alone on the corner of the street. Huge, its dark flanks solidly stuffed, locks gleaming like blank little eyes.

'Where did that thing come from?' he asked.

Amber averted her gaze. 'Probably filthy. Come on.'

'But look. It's full of stuff.'

'Could be anything,' she shuddered.

He veered towards it, and she shrieked 'Joe! It could be a dead body!'

'Could be someone off on holiday.'

'JOE!'

They saw themselves suddenly reflected on the local undertaker's plate-glass window, two short round people haloed with blonde. His hair was thinning; it had started to notice.

He tried to shut out her voice.

'JOE!'

That morning had not started well. He'd switched on the news: someone, probably us, had bombed somewhere far away.

'I don't like it,' he said.

'Why not?' she asked

'We always hit someone, that's why.'

'Rubbish. There weren't any people near it. He said it was a surgical strike. Here, Joe, you've got jam on your face.'

She wiped it, hard, and he jerked backwards.

Amber still loved Joe, of course, in a disappointed way. She wanted him to be younger. Taller, less bald, less fat. More rich. And she wanted more sex, but at suitable times, because sometimes Joe's urges were inconvenient.

Now she had come on sufferance to see what he was doing to his office. After fifteen years as a moderately successful one-man-computer-parts-and-maintenance business, based in this run-down London suburb, he wanted to change it all, utterly, and hang pictures for sale on the walls. Ask the public to come in.

'Who do you think the public is round here?' she demanded. 'Yardies with sub-machine guns murdering each other on the street, that's who. Do you really think these people buy pictures?'

'Maybe,' he said, obstinately. 'People like art, these days.'

'You wish.'

In the room at the back he showed her layers of canvases stacked against the walls like playing cards. As Joe shuffled, their colours flashed and then vanished.

'Very nice,' she said, but looked away, afraid. Was he going to leave her after twenty years?

They walked back through. Everything looked different. Sun in the front office and blank white walls where there used to be dusty rows of junked mouse-grey monitors. Panic rose in her.

Joe saw she was frowning, her eyes darting this way and that, then down, and pressing her lips together in that new way she had.

She said 'I thought galleries had upper-class gels sitting at desks batting their eyelids. You're not a gorgeous upper-class girl.'

'The artists don't care who sells their stuff. They like me, Amber. They're young ...' Her mouth shrivelled like a mollusc in lemon juice. 'Do *you* still like me?' he suddenly asked. 'We could all be killed tomorrow, with the world as it is. Do you love me, Amber? Tell me you do.'

'I'm your wife,' she said, her eyes on the floor.

The case was still standing there when they went home. It looked darker than before, now the sun had gone in. Amber swerved away.

'People are irresponsible,' she said. 'It's litter –'

'It could be packed for a holiday in Australia.'

'Could be full of guns,' she snapped. 'They should blow it up. That would make it safer.'

On Sunday they bickered again. Now the children had gone their separate ways – David to train as an accountant, Chloe to uni to read English (which wasn't exactly a practical option, but would Chloe listen to her mother?) – Amber hoped she and Joe would start staying in bed again at weekends to make love, but he always seemed to have work to do. So she had started going to church. 'Coming?'

Feeling guilty that he wasn't, he said 'Don't suppose they'll be praying for those poor people that got bombed.'

'Why should they?' she demanded, red-faced. 'It was a ... They said it was a ... you know, humanitarian bombing. You're just soft.'

He wondered when she had stopped being human.

One more artist, then Joe would be ready. There would be press, celebrities – D. Viner, the gospel sisters who'd made a CD for charity, and that sweet but alcoholic man who used to dance with Pansy's People ... It wasn't really setting his sights high enough, though, if the press launch was to make an impact. I know, he thought, Mick Jagger's daughter. The one with a jewellery business in a loft up the road. And she would come in with her famous smile and buy –

What would she buy? What would be right for her? He frowned, uncertain. One more artist, the perfect artist, that was all he needed. Tomorrow he was going to Kilburn to see Faith Upshot, from Goldsmiths, who said she liked Cultural Studies. 'Culture is, um, great,' he had replied.

Next day, some time before six when he locked up to go to Kilburn, the suitcase disappeared. There was still a dark oblong of pavement, as if the case had been full of water, and on the edge, two earwigs struggling. Joe felt bereft to see it had gone; he had somehow expected it to wait for him, as if he could open it, step in, swim away.

Faith Upshot's street was shabby, with flashes of style. An open window with a huge golden fish as a lantern, a couple of expensive cars. He rang on the last of four sellotaped bells, which said 'Upshot' in flying black letters. She would be waiting inside, excited and nervous.

He rang again, feeling powerful.

Stiletto heels came charging downstairs like a clatter of falling trays. She opened the door out of breath, faintly dishevelled, with red bruised cheeks and lips.

But she smiled with perfect poise, and said 'I'm Faith,' sticking out one purple-tipped hand. She had a strong jaw and big dark-pupilled eyes, and she talked in an endless disjointed stream. She wore a tiny denim skirt, violet fishnets, scarlet high heels, a purple teeshirt with a diamante beer mug on the front.

The paintings were possibly, as she said herself, gesturing towards where they were ranged in a row on her bed, 'not quite there yet'. Tangled green abstract landscapes, he saw, textured with real grass or straw. 'Raffia', she told him, with a little laugh, as though raffia was outrageously funny. 'What do you ...? I think they're, I don't know, you know, there's a dialectic of self I haven't quite ... like, it's a socially constructed thing ... and it's gendered, very gendered work, which is not to say ... I'm not an essentialist. You're not an essentialist, are you?' It was a foreign language to him. 'Tracey Emin', he found himself saying, unaccountably, then stopped.

'Oh *Emin*', she said. 'What can you say? She's old now. But quite nice.'

Tracey Emin old? Was she teasing him? 'Have you got anything else?' he asked anxiously, patting his bald patch, hiding it.

She was off again. 'There are these, but you see they objectify the tension between being and becoming, I don't know if you'd like to, I don't know if anyone can, they're hard to ...' She pulled him by the hand into her tiny kitchen.

He loved them at once. They were small polished suitcases made out of shiny paper she had worked to look like leather, with miniature labels, miniature chalk marks from Customs, miniature leather tags, tiny bright locks no bigger than the purple fragment of nail on her little finger. He touched one with wonder.

'Do they open up?'

'You see that's not the ... Obviously it's more about the tension between the inner and the outer, which questions –'

'I think they're beautiful.'

On the day of the opening he closed the office at midday, and Amber, who had taken the day off, came in to help him set up. She had baked cheese straws and anchovy tarts and had brought some crudités to make up on the spot.

Somebody rapped on the window. 'Later,' Joe mouthed elaborately through the glass, at two Asian teenagers who giggled and made vigorous up-and-down motions with their hands, then ran away. But by five the pictures were all hung, and Faith's beautiful cases were displayed on shelves, invisibly wired in place. By six Amber had taken off her apron to reveal a black stretchy top which showed her breasts

'I like some of these,' she said, gazing around her. 'You always had a good eye.'

'But *you* had a marvellous eye.'

They looked at each other, and smiled. At six ten, the first punter came in.

At nine-forty-five, they stood shining-eyed and exhausted, watching Faith Upshot depart at last with the younger D. Viner sister, who looked stunned. 'Which interrogates plenitude and difference, *obviously*,' Faith confided in her, then mouthed over her shoulder to Joe, 'Look I'm over the moon, she bought *three*!'

'That was brilliant,' said Amber, locking the door. 'I've taken six hundred and thirty pounds.'

Joe riffled her hair, which was glossy and dark with sweat. 'You looked wonderful. I was proud of you. Let's have a drink,' he said, refilling their glasses.

Suddenly someone was there at the window, waving a notebook. It was the reporter from the *Harlesden Harrier*, come late. He seemed keener on the drink than the story.

'I don't suppose anyone exciting was here?'

'Freddie Frame,' Joe started. 'He used to dance with Pansy's –'

'Mick Jagger's daughter,' Amber suddenly interrupted, laying one hand seductively on the reporter's arm.

He began to write furiously. 'Did she buy anything?' he asked.

'Yes', Amber replied with a dazzling smile. 'Oh, and Damien Hirst. That was quite a coup for us. And, you know, Tracey Emin.'

'Tracey Emin,' he said. 'Wow. That'll do it.'

After he wove away, Joe found one of Faith's suitcases lying on its own behind the counter. 'Love these,' he said. 'How many did we sell?'

'That's ours,' she said, blushing. 'Yours. I bought it for you. I actually like it a lot. Though she talks the most awful rubbish.'

He remembered, in an instant, why he loved her.

After midnight, they were sprawled naked on the bed, dozing. Joe reached out beside the bed and found the marvel she had given him, the beautiful miniature suitcase with its *trompe l'oeil* locks and labels, stroking it, slipping the lock, and then it was yielding, swinging up, and he saw, he saw ...

Amber lay with a soft dark V of shadow opening towards the television, where she had flicked on the twenty-four-hour news.

There were shots of bodies sprawled every which way by the bombs. 'Poor people,' she said, 'poor people,' pulling the duvet up slowly, tenderly to cover their bare limbs.

Righteousness

May bumped towards June in a fever of wind that switched, without warning, into mugginess, so old women sweated and fought off their cardigans. Next morning, though, they were shivering again as katabatic gusts swooped down over Europe, and out in the country, horses snorted and fretted and stamped up and down, swooshing their tails.

'I suppose,' said Molly in the charity shop, doubtfully, since she didn't know geography, 'this wind must come from Russia or Poland, it can't be the Arctic, since that's all melting. I never remember it as cold as this.' Opposite the 'Rumanian Orphans' shop-window a white lilac had been browned by the rain and the blooms shook furiously like dirty feather dusters.

Molly didn't know what stock to display. She put away the woollies, then dragged them out again. The punters were fractious, and would not buy summer dresses.

'Takings are down, with this mad weather,' she said, but cheerfully, to Isaiah.

He had stood outside the shop for a year or more, telling people about the end of the world. There was a kettle at the back of the shop, and she sometimes made him a cup of tea. She'd found, since she started doing this, that Isaiah's shouting bothered her less. And some of the words were beautiful. 'We fade as a leaf.' Yes, she thought. We could go any time, any of us. We fade as grass, or leaves, or blossom. 'Our righteousnesses are as filthy rags.' They brought her their rags, and she did her best. All sorts of things sold, even underwear. (Though Molly dreaded the complaints and the anger. Some of the regulars were the worst, like that busty young woman in the Animal Rights teeshirt. What was her name? Something pretty – Cressy – which didn't go with her cross expression. After paying twenty pence, she'd come back for a refund. Still, Cressy was poor, and a job seeker, so Molly sometimes took pity on her.) Outside the glass, the wind surged and relented.

Hector ground his teeth as the bus braked once more and the branch of a plane tree thumped the window like a weapon. Why was he wearing his stupid leather jacket?

An hour ago, the day had been chilly and wild, but now this double-decker was a box of sour heat.

When he got on with the dog, silly remarks had been made, like 'Hope you got a big pooper-scooper!' The toy dog was nearly as big as he was, and its nylon fur was hot and prickly. Its huge brown eyes gazed blankly back at him; its great floppy paw was skimming the ground, and he snatched it up, swearing, before it could get dirty. No one sat next to him and the toy dog. Hector was glad; he had a mission.

His blood was still pounding from the row with his wife. If they were *his* kids, these things wouldn't happen. He and Annie had taken the boys to the funfair, where they ran into her cocky kid brother, Jake. Although Hector was a fantastic shot, the guns on the rifle-stall were all fixed, so he'd spent twenty pounds and won bugger all. Then the boys' Uncle Jake sauntered up for a go, and by a total fluke, scooped the big Dalmatian. 'We don't want it,' Hector had told him, but Annie just said 'Of course we do,' though the kids were obviously too old for it. So Hector took it off them, as was only right, and announced it was going to the charity shop. Those boys had to learn, and he would teach them. He spotted the sign: Rumanian Orphans.

'Lovely,' said Molly to the tall, handsome man who shouldered through the hangers in his leather jacket, dragging a huge shiny black and white dog which would look an absolute picture in the window. 'Isn't it sweet?' she called to her customers, the halt, the lame, the young, the foreign, but the Animal Rights girl screwed up her face. 'That IS nice of you,' Molly said to Hector, 'brand new, as well, by the looks of it. We could charge ten, maybe twenty for something like that. We make a lot of money for the kiddies, you know.' She saw his frown relax a little.

On his way out of the shop, three things happened to Hector.

A big-breasted girl touched him on the sleeve and said, quite loudly, 'You shouldn't wear leather. It's dead animal skin,' and before he could tell the fat slag to get lost,

Isaiah built his sermon to a deafening crescendo as he walked into the shop for his cup of tea, 'as RAGS, yeah brother, and we fade AS A LEAF', spitting out the words into Hector's face, and

a man came through the door with something big under his coat, and the next moment, he was holding a gun, the great long dark barrel pointing at the till –

Hector was taking it in: *yes, a black man with a gun*, and his righteous anger made him dive straight for him, snatching the cold shaft so they went crashing to the ground, thus tripping up Isaiah, who clutched at a coat rack that toppled in turn, and all the women were screaming

the shop held its breath to see what happened

but after thirty seconds, no gun had gone off, and the only sounds were men grunting and thumping while Molly called 'Stop it, I won't have fighting.' In the end they stopped, exhausted and vaguely embarrassed, and heard her say 'Look, it's only a toy.' Then the man who had brought the toy rifle in under his coat got up, with dignity, and said 'It's madness. I bring the thing in because I don't believe in them, I don't want my children having toy guns! And see what happens. The world's gone mad.'

'I'll make some tea,' said Molly, swiftly. 'I blame the weather. Calm down, everyone.'

'Sorry,' said Hector. 'But he looked like a robber.' He picked up the dog and clutched it for comfort.

'Better than looking like a wanker, mate,' said the man he had attacked, but quietly, so only Cressy heard it, and she broke into a smile. Molly thought, that's the first time I've seen her look happy.

'Would you like a job?' she asked. 'A tenner a day?'

'But I won't sell leather. Or shoes,' Cressy bargained.

'In this life, you just have to do what's needed,' Molly sighed, picking up a tangle of shirts.

Isaiah intoned 'We are all unclean, and our righteousnesses are as filthy rags –'

'Yes yes, Isaiah, but lend us a hand, we'll just get everything back on the hangers,' said Molly, firmly, and though he shuddered to touch the leavings of frail human bodies, the prophet finished his tea, and obeyed, and slowly, the others joined in and helped, and the mad wind left them, and they were in summer.

The Good Hope

It was the last day of Joe and Amber's end of summer treat. A bargain 'late break', Joe had found on the Internet. Joe wasn't mean, he had never been mean and he loved 'abroad', but you had to be realistic. Business had gone downhill of late. Computer Dog was just treading water, it got harder and harder to be independent, with PC World and the high street chains flogging wrap-around three-year guarantees. As for his other dreams, the dreams they had shared, of their becoming art dealers, well ... Joe no longer much liked to think about those. They had needed more contacts, more finance, more help. They were little people. The world didn't care. Joe had asked around, but no one listened.

He had been awake since seven o'clock, and had taken a solitary walk around the harbour. Cool early sunlight slanted on the water, making a radiant way on the sea. He wished that Amber was here to see it: so much of life was still before them. The little yachts shone, gleaming, deserted. The owners painted their

The Good Hope

It was the last day of Joe and Amber's end of summer treat, a bargain 'late break' Joe had found on the Internet. Joe wasn't mean, he had never been mean, and he loved 'abroad', but you had to be realistic. Business had gone downhill of late: *Computer Doc* was just treading water. It got harder and harder to be independent, with PC World and the high street chains flogging wrap-around three-year guarantees. As for his other dreams, the dreams they had shared, of their becoming art dealers, well ... Joe no longer much liked to think about those. They had needed more contacts, more finance, more help. They were little people. The world didn't care. Joe had asked around, but no one listened.

He had been awake since seven o'clock, and had taken a solitary walk around the harbour. Cool early sunlight slanted on the water, making a radiant way on the sea. He wished that Amber was here to see it: so much of life was still before them. The little yachts shone, gleaming, deserted. The owners painted their

dreams on the side: *Free Spirit, Blue Bird, Indian Summer*. One
name appealed to him: *The Good Hope*. He had never been to
the Cape of Good Hope. It cheered him, though, that someone,
somewhere had thought that 'hope' was a good name for a boat.
A neat little cruiser, pale blue, chrome gleaming, anchored very
near their hotel.

Back in their room, Amber still dozed. He tried to get her to
come out on the balcony so he could show her the pretty boat.

'Come on darling, take an interest.'

'I need my breakfast,' Amber yawned.

'Please, darling, take a look.'

'I've got to have my breakfast, Joe.'

'Why Ramsgate?' she asked, when he first told her. 'I do like
abroad. I mean, even Spain.'

But Ramsgate was lovely. Very English, they thought. Georgian
terraces on top of low cliffs, a wonderfully elaborate Victorian
seafront with carved red brick and bright swags of flowers,
geraniums, petunias, lobelias, scarlet, purple, white, pink, mauve.
And pebble-free sand, and a gently shelving sea. Pink-skinned
families gambolled in the sunlight.

'There's not a lot here,' she complained, quite mildly.

'There's Thai, or French,' he said. They both liked food.

'I don't mean that. I mean ... What shall we do?'

Joe said 'At least we've got some time together.'

'But we're always together, Joe. I want an ice-cream.'

He went off promptly and bought her one. A two-ball gelato,
Green Apples flavour, which made her gasp with pleasure as

she licked and sucked. Joe watched the pink tip of her tongue, working. Did she still love him? Did she see him, or hear him?

Women tended to be inward-looking. Whereas Joe was more *au fait* with the world.

He wanted her to see that each moment counted, each one was a bonus, in the age they lived in, where death could arrive through a misunderstanding, through hatred they hadn't even seen or known about.

The sun was shining on their last day.

At breakfast, he read the *Telegraph* while she worked methodically through the guidebook.

'There's a grotto in Margate. The Shell Grotto ... Apparently, it could be Phoenician.' She wasn't quite sure how to pronounce 'Phoenician'.

'Phoenicians in Margate? Oh, trade, I suppose.' Joe's head went down into his paper again.

'What are you reading?'

'About the Twin Towers. Anniversary thing. Goes on a bit.'

'I hate all this stuff in the papers,' she said. 'It makes it all so ... real, somehow. Brings it all back. Those tiny people. You think, what can have gone through their minds? Before they jumped. Knowing what would happen.'

'*Shh*', Joe winced. He'd spotted some Arabs eating cereal not far away across the quiet dining-room. Three youngish boys, a mother in a headscarf. The father had shiny dark hair, a light suit. 'There's a Viking ship at Pegwell Bay,' Joe said, tactfully changing the subject. 'They've got the pamphlets in Reception. And a nature reserve.'

But she continued, impervious: 'I don't think I'd be brave enough to push myself off. That moment when you go over the edge –'

'*Please, Amber, there are Arabs, over there.*'

'They aren't Arabs, they come from Southall. And the woman is English. We were chatting in the Leisure Club. About the kids, and so on. She was very impressed with Chloe's job.'

Joe had a closer look when they passed the table, and the women's eyes under her heavy scarf were a calm pale blue, and he caught a scrap of talk: 'Why can't *I* steer the boat? Mum? Mum?'

'Because you're not old enough. Unless Abu says so.'

'More coffee, Mrs Khan?' the waiter asked her.

Joe and Amber decided on Pegwell Bay, or rather Joe decided for Amber.

On the way out they passed the Khan family getting dressed up in the foyer. The children were excited, shrieking with laughter. '*Abu! Abu!* Can I steer the boat?' They were wearing bright yellow oilskins, except for the mother, who still wore her headscarf. She smiled at Amber, and said 'Have a good day.'

'Hope the sea's nice,' Amber replied. To Joe she said 'I do miss them, you know. It was always fun, when the kids were here.'

'I think it's special that it's just us two.'

But her eyes were searching around the lobby.

Joe and Amber sat at the front of the bus. It was already afternoon.

'Did she take that thing off in the Leisure Club?' he asked Amber, who was pale with sun-cream.

'Who? Oh, you mean Mrs Khan. Why does her headscarf thingy upset you? She didn't take it off, she was just watching her boys. In any case, she says she can't swim. Apparently they're mad about sailing. She's a brave woman to go along.'

'Seems a bit odd, Arabs sailing,' said Joe. 'I suppose we don't actually know any, though. Or Jews, either. Of course, they're just people.'

'Well spotted, Joe.'

Amber could sound sharp.

The Viking Ship was very easy to find. It was set in concrete in a clearing by the road, an enormous wooden boat lined with coloured shields.

'It's not real though, is it,' Amber said.

'Read the notice,' he invited her. 'Men rowed this actual boat over from Denmark in 1949, and left it here. Sort of re-creation. But it was still real.'

Joe felt suddenly cold in the wash of sunlight. The men who had done it must now have grown old. Behind this ghost ship were all the others, rowed by real Vikings, a thousand years ago. How brave they had been, the old invaders. Pushing blindly off the edge of the world. It took such courage. Could he have done that?

'So where's this nature reserve?' Amber asked. Joe peered through the bushes with his binoculars, and got a fuzzy close-up of a crisp packet.

Leading away from the road, a path took them over a railway line overgrown with brambles. They came to wide rafts of weed-scattered concrete. Silky-eared grasses grew up through the cracks. Beyond them, shallow sea, and sandflats.

No people anywhere. It was very quiet, except for the distant drone of the road. Suddenly Joe heard birdsong.

'It's some sort of dump,' Amber decided.

'I think I get it,' Joe said, slowly, reading a faded notice on a wall. 'This was where the Hovercraft used to land. Do you remember the Hovercraft? Once it was the fastest way to get across from France. The local council must have left it like this. Just left nature to sort it out.'

'It's not what I'd call a nature reserve,' said Amber. 'I was imagining, you know, flower-beds ...'

'That's not nature,' Joe pointed out.

'It's depressing here,' said Amber, with a shudder. 'It's as if humans have gone extinct. And it's just you and me. Just you and me left.'

'If you were the only girl in the world,' Joe sang, and went down on one knee to Amber. But she didn't laugh, and the concrete hurt his kneecap.

'I like it here,' Joe said. 'It's history. Just as much as the Viking Ship.' Blue butterflies hovered over the nettles.

'But I wanted to go to the Shell Grotto,' she said.

'Don't those Vikings mean anything to you, Amber? They're – British history. They turned into us ... Better than Margate. It's a girl thing, grottos,' said Joe, kissing her, trying to make a joke of it, but she turned away, so his mouth was full of hair, dry pale hair, tasting bitter, of perfume.

'The grotto was *Phoenician*,' Amber protested. 'I don't want to waste our last day on this.'

'Stay here with me,' Joe said, taking her hand. 'No one can see us. We can do what we like. We could swim with no clothes on. We could make love.'

She frowned. For a moment, she looked like her mother.

'We're not too old,' he said. Tears came to his eyes. 'We mustn't quarrel. It's our last day. You get a bus to Margate. Meet up later.'

'You don't mind?' she asked, docile again. She flung her arms round his neck, and kissed him. 'I won't stay long, Joe. I'll come back here and find you.'

Left alone, he felt hurt, at first, but soon that yielded to silent happiness.

Blackberries ramped along the derelict fence, hot little black and red knots of sweetness with a tart edge, a tinct of winter. All their history was tangled together: a few pink and yellow flowers still clung, and the berries were growing at every stage from yellow-green to maroon to fat black. Joe got blue stains on his white shirt, and was briefly glad Amber had gone.

He scrambled down to the little bay. It seemed to be covered with small white stones, but when he got closer, he found they were shells; Joe crunched over layers of white paired butterfly shells. Colonies of shellfish must live and die here. The hum of bees mixed with the road's low murmur, a sleepy, happy, late summer sound. Joe thought, if I died here, no one would know, and at the same moment, a piercing gladness to be alive poured through his veins. The light bounced off the white concrete, flooded from the water, poured from the sky, the amazing bowl of silver-trailed sky a tiny plane was snailing across, and Joe watched the contrail transforming itself, a ribbon of silk that unfurled, flowered outwards, was complex and dazzling as the milky way ... There was some pattern he was on the verge of grasping: it dazzled him, it lifted him up; they were almost part of it, he and Amber: his love for her, her love for him, and the ghostly Vikings, and the plane, and the grasses, the blowing grasses, the passing of things, the shells in the bay and the Shell Grotto, the blue-eyed woman with the veil at breakfast, the inexorable brambles pushing their sweet fruit up over the concrete, away to the sea ...

Yes, I understand it all.

Warm and weightless, he lay down and slept.

When he woke up, the light had deepened to the old gold of late afternoon. He ate chocolate from his pocket and sat with his binoculars, dipping and swooping out over the sea, suddenly zooming in on large heads of seagulls, greedy yellow beaks, implacable pupils, dive-bombing earthwards, too fast for him. There was a sand spit in the far distance: the binoculars picked out a tiny family, pulling something into, or out of, the water. He changed the resolution: it was a boat. Three children in yellow and two bigger figures, one of them with a towel on his head. Or her head, it might be, but they had pushed off: one of the yellow children was steering: they rocked away into the dim distance.

He sat and stared as the sky changed colour. Time expanded; it became endless. *Nobody would ever die ...*

The chill of night blew in off the sea. He started to worry. Where was Amber? It was fully dark, and the stars were up, when he heard her thrashing through the brambles, calling.

'Amber, love! I'm over here!'

Their kisses on meeting had real passion. 'Joe, darling. The grotto was fantastic. It's an underground temple. Completely pagan. Fantastic pictures all made of shells. You know, fertility symbols, and flowers, and a tree of life, and suns, and stars ... They must have been, you know, fantastic, the Phoenicians.'

'Fantastic,' Joe echoed, glad she was happy, kissing her cheek, her neck, her ear.

'Can you see stars through your binoculars?' she asked him, and began to look. But something lower down caught her eye. Single red rockets were shooting up into the air from the middle of the sea.

'Where are those coming from?' she said. They fell strangely slowly, in suspended motion.

Something unpleasant occurred to Amber. 'Take a look. Please, Joe. It might be, you know, distress rockets. People in trouble.'

'Flares,' Joe corrected her. 'I'm sure it isn't. Let's go home. I want my supper. It's only fireworks.'

'Please have a look, Joe.' But he had walked on. Sighing, Amber followed him.

They waited till ten for a bus to arrive.

'Where did the Phoenicians come from?' she asked. Joe knew more about the world than she did.

'Somewhere in the Middle East, I think ... could have been

Syria, come to think of it.'

'Fancy Syrians living here. What if they got together with the Vikings?'

'Honestly, Amber, your history is *hopeless*.'

Next day, everything was over. They woke late, and packed quickly. The eggs were cold in the grey morning light and the staff seemed rushed, with downcast faces. No one offered them a second cup of coffee. The Muslim family were not at breakfast.

'I hope they had a good day,' said Amber. 'Nice woman. I've forgotten her name.'

They were cutting it fine for the ten o'clock train. Joe had an appointment in the afternoon, a woman whose hard disk had packed up with a romantic novel on it, almost finished. She was convinced it would make her rich, if only Joe could mend her computer.

There was some kind of major hold-up in Reception. A huddle of men who smelled of cigarettes. A policeman was standing by the desk, a radio crackling on his shoulder. Then Amber saw the receptionist was crying. She was actually crying as she answered the phone. The words Amber caught were 'Mrs Khan ... very nice lady ... no, it's awful.'

'Excuse me,' Joe said, 'We do have to pay. We've got a train to catch at ten.'

'The Press are here,' the policeman was saying.

'It's the children I'm sorry for,' another voice said. 'Poor kids. They say the mum couldn't swim.'

No one took any notice of Joe. They were saying something about a boat, all talking at once, as if it was important. They didn't seem to hear him, they couldn't see him.

'Please,' he said, 'we need some help. Would you mind?'

But no one came.

Good People

Justine wondered, what is the good of these people?

Ten minutes to take-off. They were running late. To Justine, the plane smelled slightly of burning. (She had asked the stewards several times for an aspirin, but they were busy fussing with the old and the young, pillows for two ancient tortoises with sticks, colouring books for two fractious children, one of whom didn't seem quite normal. It wasn't pleasant; she looked away.)

The man came down the gangway at the edge of her vision, hauling his flight-bag, short jacket, lean hips. She sent a silent text message, *sit by me*. It was a nine-hour flight home. She had missed her husband badly while writing her piece on 'Unseen Kampala'.

As the stranger grew nearer, scanning the seat numbers, his image snapped into sharp focus. Hair very black for the colour of his skin. Dark as his sunglasses. Skin taut. Jaw clenched.

He took the window seat beside her. The smile he gave her was formal, wary. 'Excuse me, ma'am.' He took off his glasses. Sharp against the African sun in the window, the line of his cheek was a clear white cliff. His forehead was remarkably clear and unlined. Older than she thought, perhaps.

'We are waiting for a final check on a successfully replaced component in one of the turbines,' the captain crackled on the PA system. 'I hope we can still make our scheduled arrival time in London. Some high winds today but they should be behind us.'

The smell of burning seemed stronger, but she ignored it.

'How long have you been in Uganda?' she asked.

'Long enough,' the man answered. 'What a country.'

'I liked it,' she said. 'I loved the people.' Now he had come, her headache was going, though the snot-covered child was still wailing in the arms of one of the blandly smiling stewards.

'Oh there are good people,' he agreed. 'I was lucky enough to work with some very good people.'

'This year was my first time in Africa,' she offered. His teeth were very white and even.

Half an hour later they were still on the tarmac. The captain had announced the engineer's arrival. The two stewards were bent over a Ugandan mother with big twin babies who were crying lustily. No one had remembered to bring her aspirin. Reassuring music on a faintly snagged tape puffed cloudlets of travel, escape, romance, into the warm air above their heads.

The economy seats seemed very close together. She was inches away from the stranger's lean thighs. She wondered, craning round for a second at the tens of human beings, belted in, pacified, but buzzing very faintly with desire and frustration, what would happen if suddenly they all released themselves, curled into pairs and made love to each other? She found herself remembering the fault in the turbine. No one could leave now. The great doors were fastened.

The man had been talking; Justine only half listened. There was something slightly odd about the skin under his ears. Money had been stolen from his hotel room, one of the hundred-dollar bills in his jacket.

'Of course, they're poor,' she interrupted. 'It must be hard to see so many rich foreigners.' She saw his mouth twitch with impatience.

'Way I see it, there's right and wrong. If we blur that line, we all get confused. And the Bible can help us with –'

'What do you do?' she interrupted again. The plane was quivering, gathering itself. The strange child pealed with eerie laughter. She heard a steward say 'Good boy' as he hurried past to his position for take-off.

'Pardon me? I'm a freelance evangelist.'

Suddenly the engine note screamed to a climax and they were roaring full-tilt down the runway. The nose rose steeply into blue heaven.

'A freelance evangelist? Oh, I see.'

Perhaps stung by her tone of voice, he began telling her what he had been doing. 'I was working with Mrs Museveni's people. You know, the president's wife? They're good people, around Janet.' The project had been AIDS education.

Justine rushed to show she could relate to this. 'It's so impressive, how Uganda is handling it. AIDS posters all over the place. Were you encouraging them to use protection?'

'Well, first of all, let's get the basics straight. See, I believe the Bible is the Word of God. And the Bible tells us to be pure until marriage –'

'I respect what you're saying,' she said, untruthfully, and raised her voice slightly, putting him right. 'But the reality is, young people have bodies, and their bodies push them in a certain direction.'

'And their souls, ma'am? Shouldn't we be saving their souls?'

The molten lake. The dark flames of hell. She drew a deep breath and prepared to refute him, but the captain came on, sounding cheerful and English. A little light turbulence: fasten your seat-belts.

They sat in silence, turned away from each other. The seat-belt sign went off again. Then the lunch trolley pulled them in the same direction. She wanted the wine, but she didn't want him judging her. 'Just water, please,' the evangelist said. The stewardess had a kind, tired face. The plane juddered and she lurched sideways. 'Are you okay Ma'am?' the evangelist asked. A steward came and helped his colleague straighten her trolley, where a dozen little bottles had toppled over, and patted her uniformed arm, consoling. The seat-belt indicator flicked back to life.

Angrily, Justine snatched the red wine, giving the small bottle a rather silly flourish. *I don't have to be a good girl any more.* Once she'd taken a deep drink, she was ready to confront him. 'Did you say Janet Museveni? The president's wife? They say the government is deeply corrupt. Wasn't it a problem working with them?'

His expression of annoyance came slowly, with effort, as if it was pulling against bands of tight tissue, as if his whole head was muscle-bound. 'What I can tell you is that these are good people. All the people round Janet are saved.'

Justine sat there watching him drink his water and read his book: *The Fire this Time.* The sun had moved, and fell directly on him. With a little shiver of triumph and horror, she began to understand his face again, the lean, craggy jaw, the smoothed pale skin. His hair and eyebrows were carefully dyed. His features had all been shifted slightly, spring-cleaned, tightened, purified. She remembered, with a jolt, watching Ugandan TV. A snowy-haired, arthritic, spruce evangelist, a tiny moon-man who must have been near eighty, had solicited gifts of $70, more than the average Ugandan annual income. He had no lines; his eyes were badly skewed.

They're all the same, she thought. Liars. Inhuman. They will not grow old, like the rest of us.

At that moment, the plane fell out of the air.

People were screaming, and a trolley crashed past them, and something hard hit her on the shoulder. Everything was changed, in violent motion. The world left them, they began again –

their arms came together, and they clutched each other's hands, clutched and held, and the plane fell further –

flesh and bone, they gripped each other

61

she was praying to everything and nothing to save her, to some God of love who cared if she fell, to anyone who loved her, to the universe, the great blue unsteadiness outside their thin shell, but it was her neighbour's hand that held her, and she held him –

then the plane stopped falling.

In the relative silence, someone was moaning. A child, or a woman, began to cry. A stewardess lay half under a trolley. The lockers had spewed forth some of their bags. But the engines were still working. There was no fire. Remarkably few people seemed to be hurt. Her neck felt bad, but she could look around. The plane moved confidently through bumpy air.

Now the captain came on to reassure them, sounding out of breath, but more English than ever. Sorry he had not seen that coming. Fortunately able to pull her up again. 'I gather there's some cleaning up to be done, but I hope you will enjoy the rest of the flight.' There was scattered clapping; one man shouted 'Well done.' Then the volume of talk became deafening. Two stewards, glistening with perspiration, something wild about their pupils, came down the aisle, checking who was hurt, calming people down, handing out bandages and consolation.

Justine and her neighbour remembered they were touching, and smiled at each other, washed clean by terror, and gingerly let each other go.

'Thank the Lord,' he said, but his voice was different, his pressed blue shirt black with sweat.

Garrulous with relief, she began to tell a story. All round the plane, people turned to each other, talked about what was important to them, the things they had felt in the dying moments which had suddenly, sweetly lifted back into living.

'What you said about the thief who took your hundred-dollar bill. Nothing like that ever happened to me. But one day I got on the wrong *matatu*, and it dropped me off in a rough part of Kampala ... I was being jostled in a crowd of people, and suddenly an old woman pressed up close to me and shouted, in English, "She's with me! She's with me!" and put her arm around me, and said "That youth want to take your bag", and pointed to a thin boy running away. Then she walked with me to some better streets. She did all that to help a stranger. I said "God bless you" from the bottom of my heart. When she left me she asked "Are you saved?" And you know, I'm not religious the way you are,' (she smiled, tried to catch his eye) 'but I told her "Yes," because she *had* saved me.'

The evangelist shifted, his face a reproof. 'But Ma'am, excuse me, you are not saved.'

'It was a white lie,' Justine cried, indignant.

'It was false witness,' he insisted.

Her voice rose shrilly in self-defence. 'But when the plane was falling, weren't we both praying? What about love? That woman showed me love.'

Then, angered by the haloes of ice in his eyes, neat in their tight new wallets of skin, she reached out and took his hand again, reached out and locked his fingers in hers, palping him to warmth as he resisted, and he pulled away restrainedly, because she was a woman, but she held him, mercilessly, making him love her, and after a bit she saw he was weeping, but Justine held on, sure she was right, converting him, forcing him to see she was a good person.

(And hidden by their uniforms, unquestioning, the faithful stewards worked on in the background, quietly doing whatever was needed.)

The Money

My driver – people with drivers always say 'my driver' – arrives looking immaculate, in maroon African shirt and shiny black trousers. This morning he is smiling an especially brilliant smile, because we are going to his village.

We have agreed the money, but there's something that he wants to explain. 'My wife is in the jeep,' Magomu says. 'I hope this is okay with you.'

I say 'Yes'. After all, we are going to the village. The wife will like it, the village will like it.

'You remember I have two children?' Magomu asks.

I say 'Yes'.

'The children are in the jeep,' Magomu tells me.

So everyone is in the big silver Japanese four-wheel-drive I am hiring for the day – the wife, the baby, naked in a neat snow-white cloth nappy, the three-year-old, big-eyed in a red American sweat-shirt. They are all in holiday mood, and so am I. The sun is shining, and we are off to the village.

First I ask Magomu a favour, though. It's always best to ask before you take pictures, though if you give money, there's usually no problem.

'Magomu, may I take a picture?'

'Of course,' he says.

So I photograph the family, mother and father smiling, children watchful, big-eyed. Gotcha!

'I'll be able to take pictures in the village?' I ask.

'Of course.'

'That's marvellous.'

Everything is settled.

As we drive through the steep potholed streets of Kampala, severely shorn teenage girls are flocking to church, slender brown calves protruding from the generous hems of elaborate, multi-layered frocks in fruit-drop colours, yellow, pink, lacy, be-ribboned. In London the respectable teenage daughters of doctors and policemen and teachers all dress like pole-dancers, but never in Uganda. At a Kampala schools concert, to which I was taken by Museveni's people, HIV was personified as a devil that the cast attacked with spears. I smile approvingly at these teen queens' pretty, safe, infantilising dresses.

'Life here is much more innocent than London. People seem happier.'

'You are happy?' Magomu's wife asks from the back. She smiles at me. This is going well.

Now we are out in the countryside. Magomu hoots magisterially, from our great silver height, at the push-bikes wavering along in our path with their pillioned, side-saddle mothers and babies, their toppling ten-foot bundles of firewood, their huge hooked anchors of *matooke* or green bananas under which the lean black legs of the seller stick out, pedalling frantically. I write all the details in my notebook.

People stop and stare at the *muzungu*, the white person, roaring past. Ugandans used to think the white was painted on, that we weren't real.

(I wonder if I am, entirely real. This time tomorrow, I'll be on a plane home, floating in my own cool pressurised dreamtime, starting to forget them, if I'm totally honest.)

But tomorrow feels a long way away. Today Uganda is hot and intimate and all-around me, fertile, glorious. Sun makes everything glow and burn. By the roadside, women are selling pyramids of tomatoes, yellow-green speckled monster jackfruit, pineapples, avocadoes, pawpaw. A rich country, a beautiful country. Surely no one here can go hungry.

'It might rain,' says Magomu, indicating the blueing and darkening of the clouds ahead.

Now we are bouncing along red unsurfaced roads, which give way, eventually, to a narrow track. Nearly there. I want to know Magomu better.

'In my family there were three of us,' I tell him. 'How many of you are there, Magomu?'

'Seven brothers.' He seems quiet. Maybe it is not easy going back. Petrol is dear; his mother has never seen the new baby, her grandson.

But the country here is lovely, to my eyes – hilly, open, green, uncultivated.

'It's pretty, Magomu.'

'All this was our father's land. He left it to me and my brothers.

Forty acres,' he says.

'You are a landowner, Magomu! You are rich!'

He is silent.

The track ends in a flat muddy clearing. A single brick-built house, with a tin roof. Inside there is a striking woman of perhaps my age, but very bent, in a dark red, square-necked dress. She has bare feet and a cross on a thin chain. As I stand in the doorway watching, she produces a large piece of pink patterned cotton with which she covers a sofa worn down to the wooden frame. Once we are both sitting down, she greets me, bowing, and I bow too. We vie to bow the lowest.

She speaks to me in Luganda, and Magomu translates. 'My mother is happy. She says, a white woman never came in her house before. A white woman never came in our village.'

It's quite a responsibility. 'Tell her, I am very happy, I am honoured to be here. What is her name? May I take a picture?'

'Of course,' he says. So I use my flash, which lights up the room in all its bareness.

'Now I take you to see the others,' says Magomu, leaving his wife and children with his mother, who is delighted with the baby.

We climb a narrow path through high scratchy wild palms. I am panting in the sultry heat. The malaria pills must be making me breathless. I'm glad when the sun goes in for a while.

'It will rain,' says Magomu.

Eventually we come to another house like the first. A young woman with a worn, beautiful face runs out and embraces Magomu, then tries to kneel before me, so I kneel with her, and we hug. 'My sister-in-law', says Magomu. She collects two plastic jerrycans, one huge and dark green, the other smaller and yellow. I take a picture of her with the jerrycans.

'We go to fetch water,' he says, and we set off again. I am thirsty, and hungry, but of course I say nothing. Soon we meet another thin sister-in-law, and then another, but no husbands. Children flock to join us, barefoot, running ahead and behind us, laughing, saying 'How are you?' in English, trying to write their names in my notebook.

We come out on a hillside which has been roughly hoed. The soil looks good, but most of this land is not cultivated. Why, I wonder? But there are figures on the crest of the hill. 'This is my brother,' Magomu says.

At last I meet one of Magomu's brothers. He looks much older, gravely lined, silver-stubbled. A few teenage boys move slowly down the brown and green field, sowing grey-green wrinkled maize seeds by hand.

At the bottom of the hill, a concrete sink is set into the ground, with a four-inch wide pipe, constantly running. 'Here is the water for our village,' Magomu says. 'The water for our village is very important.' So I take a picture, then another.

The first sister-in-law fills the plastic carriers. She puts the large green one on top of her head. Before she can pick up the yellow can as well, I get it myself, and set off up the hill. I want to show them I'm one of them.

'It is too heavy for you,' says Magomu.

'It's okay,' I say, but in fact, it is an effort. The boys on the field are pointing and laughing in my direction, not unkindly.

'They are saying, look at the *muzungu* carrying water,' says Magomu. 'They never saw this before. Are you tired?'

'I'm not tired,' I lie, but I am tired and hungry.

Long before we get to the top of the first hill I am panting hard and dripping sweat. Magomu takes the jerrycan from me without a word. I hope the boys in the field don't notice.

Back at the mother's house a fire has been built up in a tiny brick building at the back, the cookhouse. The mother and the sisters-in-law fill a cauldron from the jerrycan, and *matooke* is put on to boil in the flaming impossible heat. The children sit beside us on the ground, watching and brightly listening, as Magomu and I talk and the storm rumbles overhead. A neighbour comes to chat, and borrows money from Magomu. How can Magomu have money to lend? But probably pennies are riches in this village.

Eventually big raindrops start and we retreat under the corrugated eaves. Here we can no longer see the cooking. After a bit, I hear a low, regular thumping, nearby. 'Is that the drums?' I ask Magomu. (I secretly wonder if they are signalling: 'Soon we are going to eat the *muzungu*.')

He laughs a lot and takes me round the corner where a sister-in-law is bending in the rain, pounding groundnuts in a two-foot tall wooden mortar, with a long, crude, wooden pestle.

I take a picture, though she waves me away. 'She would like to be more smart,' Magomu explains, but I laugh and tell her it is quite okay, I really don't mind if she isn't smart.

Afterwards I think, perhaps *she* minded.

Lunch is served! We three guests of honour go into the house and are presented with two plates each, one of orange mashed *matooke*, kept piping hot with a banana leaf lid, the other an individual dish of pale pinky-beige groundnut sauce, both delicious. I eat ravenously. Magomu says 'I am happy you are eating.' Encouraged, I stuff myself like an intestine sausage. The children watch and laugh through the window. I tell myself not to be self-conscious. Everyone seems happy. I am happy.

Outside, the sun appears again.

Before we leave, Magomu wants to show me one more thing. 'My brothers,' he says, and gestures up another slope. We climb it. Just over the brow of the hill, I see something strange. Low, blank, white structures, one after another, shining, shining, shinging in the sun.

'My father's grave,' Magomu says.

But there are so many graves. I see a little field of grey-white light which must be very recent.

'And the others?' I ask, after a pause.

'My brothers' graves. They die of AIDS, one after one.'

'Sorry,' I say. 'So sorry.'

And it starts to fit together, the ragged children, the women without husbands, the untended fields, the exhausted older brother.

'Now you take a picture,' he says. 'You must take a picture of this, also. Take a picture.'

'Do you mean it, Magomu?' I am unsure.

'Have you got enough pictures now?' Magomu asks.

We get ready to drive back to Kampala.

Now once again there is something he wants to explain.

'You remember the neighbour you met?'

I say 'Yes.'

'The neighbour is in the jeep. I hope that is okay with you.'

I say 'Yes.'

'You remember my father had a sister?'

I say 'Yes,' although I don't remember.

And soon we are all in the jeep, Magomu and me, his wife, his two children, his neighbour and his father's sister. There are a lot of us, and everyone is in good spirits, but I'm thoughtful on the journey back to Kampala.

Tomorrow Magomu will drive me to the airport at 6 am. I put the money for the two journeys, 150,000 Ugandan Shillings, in an envelope and leave it in my hotel room. Then I go and use up my spare change on dinner. My big starchy lunch seems to have left me empty.

When I come back, the envelope with the 150,000 shillings has disappeared.

It is impossible, but true.

I stay up half the night searching, unable to believe it has gone, increasingly frantic, at 1 am, at 2 am, at 3, looking in the same few places over and over again. I cannot sleep. I lie there sweating in my stifling white shroud of mosquito net, thinking about the village, the people's generosity and cheerfulness, the water running in the concrete sink, the clever children, the missing money, Magomu's money, the money I owe him.

In the morning, I have to face my driver. Reception at the hotel is not open; it is too early. 'I hope I can change money at the airport, Magomu, but you see I've only got travellers' cheques.' Travellers' cheques are not easy to change in Uganda.

He is very sorry about the stolen money but takes me seemingly without a flicker of doubt to Entebbe, as if he really believes in me, as if the *muzungu* is to be trusted.

In the soft early light, hundreds of children are walking to school in immaculate, English-style school uniform, white shirts, navy, green or maroon v-necks, some with books balanced on their heads, looking light-hearted, hopeful, and determined as they flood onwards into the morning. They still believe in our English education, far more than English people do. I think about the ragged children in the village, and wonder, were any of them ill? Will they ever get a chance to study in the city?

Magomu, beside me, is not talkative.

Now there is no time left before I reach the airport. The sun climbs through the sky, white and blinding, inescapable, staring me full in the face. Now is the moment.

'I am afraid that once you are through check-in they will not let you come back,' says Magomu suddenly, not looking at me, not smiling.

I am afraid too, sweating coldly.

Afraid that I shall not get the money, Magomu's money, the children's money.

Afraid that I took too many pictures. That the money can never be enough. That I shall let them down. That I shall not come back.

Starting at Last

Joe was going to the garage to get started at last when his eye, looking out through his suburban window, fell on the first sun that pierced the garden. It was a short shining ribbon, a radiant way, which found the pink roundlets of quince blossom. The white and gold frills of gauze narcissi. The tight blue cones of grape hyacinth. Things he had put in once, long ago (when the children were young, and so was he), and which quietly happened year after year, undisappointing, endlessly reviving, held by their own rhythms, effortless.

'What are you doing? You haven't gone anywhere.' Her voice, hectoring. 'You see what you're like? We'll never get those shelves, Joey.'

'It's the garden,' he said. 'It's a lovely day.'

'Get on with it.'

He hated her. It was starting again, the tight band saying 'sad' that weighed down the bony wings of his ribcage. That sad bad tightness came when they argued. Because he loved, as well as hated, Amber, and couldn't leave her, but didn't please her. He

75

must not hate her, because she was right. Life was short, he must get things done.

Since he had retired – because, in the end, the office cost more than it was bringing in, because his customers were getting older, and so were their computers, which they joked were 'dying', and sometimes *Computer Doc* couldn't revive them – he had done almost nothing but wait for spring, and watch summer, and relax into the slow burns of autumn, until Amber made him sweep up the leaves. He wanted to let them lie to make leaf-mould for the worms to pull down into the beds, but she didn't like mess, and they did rot the lawn, the lawn which she shaved to green perfection, her favourite part of their little garden.

Back then in *Computer Doc*, he could have told her, he didn't look out, he couldn't feel the weather, he had no idea which season it was. That was why these days he watched, and counted. Maybe today he would explain it to Amber. He still felt life was rare and precious. He had plans, inchoate, to rebuild the garage as a studio, with a big sunny window. Amber had talent, he knew she did, and even *he* did – there could be room for both of them. There was still time, and they had his pension.

But Amber just nagged him to build more shelves. If they had enough shelves, their life would be tidy. Whereas Joe was afraid shelves would make their life smaller. He'd noticed she no longer read the newspaper.

'It's a lot of money and there's so much rubbish.'

'Yes, but there's a big world out there, Amber. Wars, and viruses, and global warming. You used to be interested in things.'

'I'd rather put my own house in order.'

He'd had four years of freedom since retiring. Four springs, four summers, four gold and red autumns. Winters they turned in on themselves and quarrelled, but spring came round again, a miracle. Bulbs, to him, were magical things, hiding their fire in their folded layers, buried in the dark, unattended, holding their warmth year after year, then the generous, impromptu uncurling of colour, the fuse with its spark of life racing outwards, each time a new, tangential unfurling, a different wonder of leaf and flower. Their outsides, like his, were shabby and flaky, papery, peeling layers of skin, but underneath, the fire hid and waited.

He would do it at last. He would get started.

'I'm doing it,' he said, with an edge of anger. 'I'll get it done, you know I will.'

But the look Amber gave him seemed sour and scornful. 'Before both of us die, I hope,' she said.

'Why do you have to talk about dying?'

His brother had died two months ago. It had seemed impossible, unbearable that a brother of his, from his generation … Alan had been the first one to go.

She came and stroked his shoulder, briefly. 'Sorry, Joe. Love you, dear.'

He thought, she doesn't. She doesn't love me.

'I wish you loved me,' he said, sadly. 'I thought we'd be so happy, with both of us home. All those things we wanted to do.'

'We have been happy,' she said, surprised, and came back again, and kissed his cheek, moving into the path of the sunlight. 'Just because I want you to shelve up the garage, it doesn't mean that I'm unhappy. There's plenty of time to do all we want to.'

Suddenly he felt lighter, freer. Amber gazed at him with what was surely affection. She was looking pretty, in a plain tight sweater, her skin gleaming like a new tulip, dots of spring sun in her irises. Her hair was still more brown than grey.

'Let's go and lie down,' he said, urgently. 'How long is it since we made love?'

But her mouth pursed up, and her eyebrows creased, and she managed to look a decade older. 'You said you were going to the garage.'

'I know I did, but life is short.'

'Precisely. There's just such a lot to get done. I don't mean to reject you, darling. It's just, when you say you're going to do a thing –'

'Yes, I know.' She had been saying it all their married life: *do what you say you're going to do. Don't say it if you don't mean it.* But where did that leave dreams, and reflections? When did you get time to understand?

He turned away from the sun into the unlit room, and went to the understairs cupboard for his jacket. 'I'm going, I'm going.' His voice nagged with complaint. Even he could hear it, but he couldn't help it.

'Don't snap at me, Joe,' she said. 'It upsets me.'

'Well you upset *me*,' he grunted from the cupboard.

What chaos it was. He had promised to clear it, but decades of mess waited under the stairs, paintings he had got lumbered with, the children's sports kit, the Christmas decorations, the tangled tinsel of former happiness, things he didn't want to give up just yet, for surely it was all only yesterday, surely the ribbon of time might loop back, Chloe would suddenly dart down the hall and slip on her rollerblades in seconds and swoop and dance like a swift down the road, and he and Amber would watch her together, holding hands, proud, in the bright doorway.

'I can't hear you, Joe.' Now she was shouting.

'It doesn't matter,' he answered, and left, giving the door a curt little slam. Perhaps he had won, and he felt better. Then he thought about Amber, and felt worse. He did love her, didn't want to annoy her. She was all he had now, all that was left. His yoke-mate for the last part of the road.

But once she was my skinny, my quicksilver darling, in Portugal, on the burning sand, and she drew a bird with her toe by the water, and took off her top and plunged into the Atlantic, her cool white flesh in the bright blue waves.

The inside of the garage looked very dark as he peered through the dusty glass of the windows, and he hesitated. It would be cold. He would be in there forever, once he started. He wanted to stay in the sun for a while. She couldn't see, from the house, what he was doing. That had always been the way it worked: they had times together and times apart. Once he'd been alone for a bit, he would feel better, and go back in and be cheerful again, and perhaps, after lunch, she would come to the bedroom.

He had bought the timber for shelves last year, cheap plasterboard which would serve its purpose, but he wasn't sure that he had the right saw. He wasn't really a handy man. It was one of the many ways he had failed her. The handles fell off the drawers in the kitchen; the wrong kind of paint peeled off the doors. He had put off mending the fence too long, so finally the whole lot had to be replaced, and both timber and workmen were very expensive, and she'd said, wryly, 'That could have been a holiday.'

'We'll still have a holiday,' he had pleaded. 'I've got a credit card. Let's go back to Lagos.' Their honeymoon in Portugal, a lifetime ago.

'You're a dreamer, Joe,' she had said, with finality, and then, with half a smile, 'At least the fence is mended. We can go away to Mum's, and the dogs won't get in.' Her mother, unlike his, lived on forever, a pale widow in a suffocating flat.

He sat in the air and light, and thought. His mother-in-law was eighty-nine. She was a freeze-dried version of her daughter, tiny, bony, almost transparent, the laughter and the fluidity gone, but her worries, her fusses, reminiscent of Amber's. She lived in a complex of sheltered flats where electric scooters whined quietly down the landings until their owners could no longer use them. The flat was so small that her muscles had wasted; she liked fresh air, but was afraid of flies, and dazzled birds, and mosquitoes, and traffic noise, so kept the windows shut all year round, and sat and suffered, fighting for breath. She was looking forward to her ninetieth. This was a marathon she meant to win, shuffling down her lane looking over her shoulder at the halt and lame who were her competitors. When he and Amber came to stay, they had narrow twin beds in the cold guest bedroom, and never stayed long enough, nor did the right things, and failed to bring the children, whom she claimed to love, though whenever David or Chloe did visit, their grandmother made the young people feel guilty: 'No one ever comes to see me,' she told them. 'I know, I'm an old woman, you're tired of me.'

Yet her eyes were good. Her hearing was good. She could still smell the freesias Amber brought her, religiously, because they were her mother's favourites, because Amber still hoped to make her happy. She should have been happy to have lived so long: all those minutes, all those hours, and nothing to do but chat to her rivals, bother the warden, and play mind games with the harassed Poles and Albanians and Russians and Afghans who served her meals and changed her sheets. She *couldn't* be happy; which angered Joe, she didn't realise how lucky she was, she was always taking against people, resenting this one, offended by that one, convincing herself she was hard done by, and the band in his chest grew tighter again, for he himself had so little freedom, and had to do so many small tasks, and could never sit as she did and stare out of the window. Would never be an artist, or a millionaire, or any of the things they had once dreamed of being.

God save me from going in that flat again. The smells of air freshener and dried lavender not quite concealing the meals on wheels. Don't shut me up in there again.

Yet Joe couldn't help envying his mother-in-law, with more in the bank account than him, thirty extra years of living on this planet, and the envy turned into anger with Amber, her mother's daughter, his task-master –

But once she was twenty, and loved me so much, and made love to me in the open air, under the mimosa tree in the Algarve, and then we heard goat bells, and pulled up our clothes, so silly with laughter we couldn't get them on again.

– and Amber had suffered from her mother too. Who didn't think Joe was good enough, didn't like the way Amber brought up the children. Didn't love Amber as she deserved. As she, Amber, loved Chloe and David. She gave the love she had never received.

Amber loves our children. She says she loves me.

There was a sweet smell. A piercing smell. It was the winter jasmine, coming late this year, low growing against the foot of the house, white sweet stars a small breeze was moving. He breathed it in, and his chest felt better, his body less of a rigid prison. I'm still here inside, he told the sun. I love it out here, I love the spring, I love it all, the daffodils, the jasmine ... Tenderness made him come alive. The starred cloud of jasmine made a small milky way, leading to the promise of the blue above him. Tears sprang to his eyes, of happiness, and he thought, 'I love her, I always loved her', and that understanding was a flood of white light, for that was the point, the point of it all, and all he needed was time to tell her, and he thought, *I am going to pick her flowers, I will make a bouquet of the quince and the jasmine and offer it to her, and explain our lives*, and the sun was all round him, full in his face, as he bent into the scent and began pulling at the jasmine, which was wiry, tougher than he thought it would be, and as he bent deeper, he briefly felt dizzy, but he went on stooping in the green and the gold, he must carry it through, he would finish what he'd started, the pain didn't matter, only the love, and he fell to the earth with her flowers in his hand, so she found him there (coming out later with tea and one of the biscuits he liked, to please him), lying at the end of the short ribbon of sunlight, her favourite flowers held out towards her.

Ring-barking

A shadow passed the end of the garden. A flicker of movement, a blur of black.

She never complained, she never cried. This was the thing she tried to hold on to: her loss was not special, nor was she. she would ask no favours, bother no neighbours; no, she was English, she would be stoic. After all, the British had lost an empire. But her road, Woodbine Road where they had lived forever (although she had never liked the name, and had got up, two years ago, a committee of residents who tried to persuade the council to change it, to Vine Avenue or Flowerhill Lane) – the road where they bought their first house together, nor dreaming that it would be their last, the road where they lived was no longer British, she thought, grimly staring out of the window at the place where once she would have seen him digging, his hair thinning, his old pullover. Now there was nothing. The cold blue yew.

Then a shadow passed the end of their garden. A flicker of movement, a blur of black.

Ring-barking

A shadow passed the end of the garden. A flicker of movement, a blur of black.

Una never complained, she never cried. This was the thing she tried to hold on to: her loss was not special, nor was she: she would ask no favours, bother no neighbours: no, she was English, she would be stoic. After all, the British had lost an empire. But her road, Woodbine Road where they had lived forever (although she had never liked the name, and had got up, two years ago, a committee of residents who tried to persuade the council to change it, to Vine Avenue or Flowerfall Lane) – the road where they bought their first house together, not dreaming that it would be their last, the road where they lived was no longer British, she thought, grimly staring out of the window at the place where once she would have seen him digging, his fair thinning hair, his old pullover. Now there was nothing. The cold blue yew.

Then a shadow passed the end of their garden. A flicker of movement, a blur of black.

She could not quite define what had happened. Behind the yew, by the sycamore tree. Blacker than the still, sodden yew tree, blacker than the poisoned ground beneath. But darkly fluid, live as a breath. A kind shadow. A friend, Una thought, and her spirits lifted. Something alive.

Since her husband died, aged forty-four, stupidly young, though he was older than her, she had stayed inside, out of the light, hardly able to walk, unable to talk, paralysed by the blow that had fallen. Sawing and hacking her world to nothing, leaving her in a cast of pain. Her whole body was immobilised, her face heavy, like a mask of wood. After all, they had been married for two decades. Two decades of waking and sleeping together.

She had lost her job five years ago, when the bank closed down their local branch, and George had been a rock to her, telling her he liked to have her at home, after all he earned enough for two of them, and for children too, for at the time they were still hoping … Her new blank days had been bright with hope, hospital visits, tests, hormones, a flurry of buds and leaves and sunlight, imagined faces, the sweetness of names, doodled pet names for those faint dream-children.

Well, in the end, they never came, and five years later, George had gone. Half a lifetime of loving plans; somehow it left her here with nothing. What could she do with the life that remained? Every day she woke slowed and deadened, clinging to her thin wedding ring for comfort.

Last night, though, she had dreamed of flying. There was light, and ease, and kind unknown hands waving her off into warm blue air. Una woke knowing that something had changed.

Autumn was coming. Apples, berries. She actually made herself a bowl of porridge. Adding dried berries, which plumped and moistened. The packet promised her a long healthy life. Oats were good for arteries. She had often offered to make him porridge, but George was obstinate, and liked fried eggs, and, every so often, a smoke in the garden, although she had always told him not to. Did she feel better because she had tried? She thought she might put the radio on, and was shocked to find that the switch had grown dusty. Yes, she would have the *Today* programme. It was comforting hearing the raised male voices. *Men*, she thought, *I always liked them.*

She felt much better until the post came, a furious ramming of dull thick letters through the narrow letterbox he never replaced, though he had promised to often enough. She tore the mail open, irritably: more calculations of possible refunds she knew she would never bother to claim, though she heard George's voice whisper urgently 'Take it, Una love. Go for it.'

They made her sad: they were the wrong letters. Not enough people, she felt, had been sorry. He was a good man who had died too young. Not enough people who loved him had written. Other people's sorrow might lessen her own. Besides, he had not been ... celebrated. Some ceremony had been omitted.

So she crouched like a crab, splayed over the computer, pointlessly searching through the bars of e-mails for something with love, kindness, humour. She clicked on George's old messages. He was always so funny, so alive in e-mail, writing from the office when he shouldn't have done. But they had grown threadbare, re-read too often.

It was then that she sensed that tremor of life, that quiver of thrill from the dank autumn garden.

She looked: there was nothing, but the sun came out and lit up the amazing, viviparous belly of white Russian vine swelling over the wall, crawling up through the yew, abseiling across on to the sycamore, blazing in a crest of vivid white tendrils at the free blue sky, forty feet up, a wild gipsy climber on the rackety tree that made the lawn dark and her plants thin and sickly. George had promised to cut the sycamore down, but now she was left with it, out of control. She turned back inwards, away from the window.

Life would have been different if there had been children. Her tests were normal, so she'd always wondered ... *Might I have had them with another man?* The thought still felt like disloyalty. It must be too late for her, now, at forty. She didn't blame him. They had given up hope.

Then it flickered again, very fast, by the wall.

She made a decision. She would go upstairs and finally turn out her husband's wardrobe. Shirts which had held his dear body, jackets which had tried to keep him warm, socks that curved round his feet like caresses. *Take them all to the charity shop.* Others could use what he could not. And then perhaps she would call the council and get them to remove the bed, for she wouldn't need a double bed again. She would buy herself a new single life, half as wide, but no longer half-empty.

The bed they had shared for twenty years. She went upstairs, sat down to rest on the rose-red bedspread with its two gentle dips, lay back for a moment, feeling her wedding ring, till her fingers relaxed and she fell asleep. And once again, she dreamed of flying.

When she woke, she felt happy for the first time since the day George had his heart attack. She opened the cupboard: a pale moth flew out, and she shuddered and drew her cardigan around her. Then she thought, maybe it was his soul. Maybe I needed to let him out, and she started dragging out hanger after hanger, pulling the clothes to her, stroking them, breathing in deep George's faint male smell with the bitter little lingering of cigarette smoke, then flinging them, lightly, untidily, into two piles, one to send to the shop, one to throw out as no use to anyone. She worked speedily, and heard herself singing.

Perhaps it was because she was singing that she didn't, at first, hear the sound of the chain-saw. Until it became so loud and insistent that she stopped mid-beat and cocked her head. A pair of cream socks she had bought him for summer, nested together like pale newborn puppies, skipped from her hand to the floor, forgotten.

The saw whined and roared like an army of hornets.

Next door, of course, to the left of her, they were building an extension, had been for weeks. The couple hardly talked to her; they were too busy, with their three small children. She didn't usually much notice the noise. And yet, this time it sounded nearer than usual. It almost seemed to come from her garden.

And because she was bored, and on her own, and wanted a break from sorting George's clothes, she slipped downstairs, unlocked the back door and stepped out, dazzled, into the morning.

There was a small dark man. A man in her garden. And everything looked different. She tried to understand. A blaze of sunlight, strange piles of hacked jungle, white flowers foaming round his feet like the sea, pale green wounds on grey pillars of wood, glistening sap breaking out like sweat. But the noise had stopped. He held a chain-saw, trembling. He was short, Indian. Faintly familiar.

His mouth hung open, but he said nothing. 'What are you doing?' she said, slowly, then louder, gathering force and fury, 'What are you doing? I don't believe it! This is my garden! What have you done?'

He was backing away now, mumbling something. 'The tree was too tall. Too tall, isn't it. Always dropping leaves on roof of my shed. Stopping the sunlight off my tomatoes. Just a small cut, love, just, maybe –' He tailed off, looking as appalled as she was, the realisation of cosmic guilt darkening and fixing his gaze upon her, and suddenly nimble, he scooped up his saw, a murderous thing like a crocodile, and with a galvanic leap and scurry, his little feet scrabbling on damp brickwork, he was over the wall, he had disappeared.

Una went on shouting in her violated garden. 'How dare you!

This is an absolute outrage! This is my property! It is *monstrous*!'
She did not have to think what to say: the words poured out, the
barriers yielded, a lifetime's sense of entitlement flooded her with
furious energy.

But shouting on her own was unrewarding. Una climbed onto
a pile of wood so she could see over the wall. As her head rose above
the parapet, women were streaming out of the house. Now there
were four figures gazing at her, framed by a lawn and a vegetable
patch, all four faces frozen with fear. She instantly recognised the
wife: Mrs Patel from the Indian shop. She had never realised they
were living there. The daughters were barely teenagers, not that
she was good at guessing ages. Sweet little things, slender and
golden. Round open mouths, tiny dark circles.

'Daddy! Daddy!' Both of them were squealing.

'You have committed a crime,' she said, absurdly, hearing
that she was ridiculous. 'I am going to the police. You will be in
trouble!' A wail rose from the three females. Feeling exposed,
sticking up over their wall, Una climbed back down again as
gracefully as possible, but turned her ankle as a branch gave way,
and shouted 'Fuck, shit, *fuck.*' Had she lost moral authority?

Looking around her, she was half-relieved to see the damage
was worse than she expected. It looked as if wild beasts had been
mating. This thought made her violently angry. Yes, she decided,
she would go to the police. She would photograph the evidence
and call the police. 'I am a widow!' she called, in valediction, to
the unseen choir of female voices.

Coming back with a camera and moving in close, her body
began to do something so strange and unfamiliar that she thought
she was dying. She saw he had scored right round the trunk with

the terrible rapacious teeth of the chain-saw, a livid circle where the bark was gone, a ring-shaped wound that would steal the tree's life, watering, weeping in the acid air, and a wave of pain shot behind her eyeballs, vivid as salt on freshly torn skin. Some kind of convulsion, some fit of grief, and then she realised that she was crying. Tears rose to her eyes in a steady stream. He had ring-barked her tree, with its crown of white creeper. There was no future. It would never recover.

As she went into the house, she could still hear them moaning. The daughters were telling their father off. 'Daddy, you know you must not cut down trees. They told us at school, do not cut down trees.' Behind them was the plaint of Mrs Patel: 'My God, Pranay, what have you done? You get a new machine, you go crazy! I leave you for an hour and you commit crimes!'

Her doorbell trilled at eight that evening, too late, in these new widowed days, for anyone to call on her, so she kept the chain on, and peered through the crack, and was happy to see blue serge, silver buttons, the pomegranate face of a middle-aged policeman.

'I'm amazed you've come,' she told him, bluntly. 'I thought you'd be too busy with crack in Harlesden.'

'We try to represent all communities, Madam,' he said, with a touch of asperity, but over a cup of tea he relaxed, and gave a low whistle when she showed him her photos.

'With this kind of dispute,' the policeman opined, 'it's usually better to avoid the courts. If you like, I'll have a talk with the other parties. A word in their ear. First thing tomorrow.'

'Does talking, you know, do the trick?'

'Some people are pig-headed,' he said, sagely. 'But what do you lose if we go for it?'

Next day she woke an hour earlier than usual. Since George had died she had been sleeping late, because there was nothing to get up for, no one to bring her a cup of tea. She would lie till ten in the dark bedroom. This morning, though, something was different. Her cheek was touched by a blade of light, a wand that delicately lifted her eyelids. She lay there for a second, wondering, then realised, Yes, it's lighter than usual. Because the mad Indian attacked our tree.

At ten there was a faint ring at the door. She opened it to find them both on the doorstep, the coloured couple, looking tired and small, both of them clutching carrier-bags, their eyes fixed timidly on the hall floor. 'Apologise,' Mrs Patel hissed, audibly, poking her husband in the ribs. Una noticed the little man's thick black hair, a pelt of fur the comb had not repressed.

'Come in,' said Una. 'You had better come in.' She turned her back so they could follow her. 'Apologise, idiot,' the wife's voice whispered.

'Do you want a cup of tea?' Una heard herself ask, then added, to establish her role as victim, 'While we look at the damage in the garden. It's very bad. I was very upset.'

'Terrible, *terrible*,' groaned Mrs Patel in her husband's ear as she saw the wreckage. 'He is going mad, you know,' she confided in Una. 'It is men, you know. Just because he is buying this new machine ... I went out for an hour, I knew nothing about it, then when I came back, he has done this thing. We don't want trouble. We have never had trouble. We have been here thirteen years, and never any trouble. Then this morning the police come and ring on our door. There was a *police car* parked outside.'

'I'm sorry,' said Una, automatically. 'Well, not exactly sorry, of course,' she said quickly. But then she saw Mrs Patel was crying, two tears running down her lined olive cheeks, narrow and direct, two shining paths.

'Now my husband will apologise,' Mrs Patel said through her tears. 'He will clear everything up. He will do anything, no problem. But please do not send the police to our house.'

Una found she was holding the woman's hand. 'The daughters were crying,' added Mrs Patel. 'You understand how it is with children. My younger daughters. Their sisters are all married.' She squeezed Una's fingers. 'You also have children?'

'I was crying yesterday,' Una parried loudly, feeling the balance was getting skewed. 'You see, my husband died this summer.'

'I am sorry, very sorry,' said Mrs Patel, yielding her position instantly. 'Oh, very sorry. It is very sad.' She gave her husband a small, savage kick. Up to this point he had been totally silent. There were dark circles under his eyes. As boot struck bone, he jerked into motion.

'Very sorry, love. Very, very sorry,' he said. 'My new shed, you see. It was a bloody ballsup. The leaves from your tree got in the gutters –' He stopped with a gasp that told Una his wife had

94

landed another kick. Mrs Patel cut in, briskly. 'Tell the lady you will sort it all out. He knows what he is doing, though he seems like moron.'

'The kettle will have boiled,' Una told them. When she came back with the tea, they were sitting on the bench, showing her the contents of their plastic bags. He had been to B&Q already that morning, and bought some liquid to protect the cut bark. 'I paint it on straightaway, no messing.' His lips were as red as her unpruned rose hips. Una found herself smiling at him. His eyes were black and berry-bright. Mrs Patel had baked some honey pastries. She held them out, a supplicant. Her husband tried to take one, but she smacked his hand away.

The two women sat in the sun and ate cakes, dipping the spiced sweetmeats in milky tea, while Una talked haltingly about her husband ('George and I never had a cross word'). Mrs Patel looked surprised, but agreed ('Pranay is too timid to quarrel with me'), and Mr Patel rushed around in circles. Though he acted like a clown, he was sturdy and nimble, and soon made the garden look much better, throwing most of the lopped branches over the wall, flourishing his brush over the wounded surfaces.

Mr Patel was the last to go. As he was skipping down the hallway with his tools, avoiding the piles of George's old books which Una in that instant thought of selling, the post arrived. There was the usual dry straining, the sound of something tearing, the abortive stump of post stuck halfway in, waggling dully like a Manx cat's tail, until with the usual brutal shove the postman managed to drive it through, a damaged flurry of dead brown mail.

'Hopeless,' said Una to Mr Patel. 'It's nothing new. It's always been hopeless.'

Inspiration struck him. His eyes glowed with joy.

'It is too small,' he said. 'I know, I know everything. I am a carpenter. I will make a new one, a bigger one, for you. My friend have the bloody metal bit, no problem. No fee, of course. So all the mail can come in. I will sort you out. I know what I am doing. I am family man, I have a damn good business. The sons, they help me. Three sons, five daughters.' He swelled visibly, his pride restored.

'That would be wonderful,' said Una. 'Thank you, really. That would be great. You see, my husband –' And she started to cry. She tried again. 'My husband couldn't – Sorry to cry, Mr Patel.'

'Pranay,' he said. 'You can call me Pranay.'

'Pranay ... That's nice. What does it mean?'

'Nothing,' he said, extending a hanky that was marked with green from the bark of her trees.

'It must mean something.' She took it, gratefully, and mopped her tears, which went on flowing.

'Actually, dear, Pranay means love,' he said, standing on the doorstep, looking full into her eyes as she held the door open. She stood there thanking him, smiling and crying, and he said sorry, again and again, and waves of feeling coursed over her features like bright leaves broken by wind and rain. The more she cried, the more he said sorry, and the more he said sorry, the more she smiled, and the door blew shut as they bobbed, like dancers, the catch slipped home with them both inside; while out in the garden the Russian vine, hacked off at the root, still lifted and shook in great blowsy loops where it had briefly fallen, white petals spuming on the yew's lopped branches.

Mornington Place

In Mornington Place, in Mornington Terrace, in Mornington Street, in Mornington Crescent, there are gaps for the moon to look through. More sky here on the edge of the park (where cars get lost after dark and circle) than anywhere else in London. More sky than is right for a city pours down through the long wide swathes of the railway cutting, where bogeys shunt and groan in the night and the lost cars honk and circle. More children, too, on a summer morning, catching the shadowless Mornington sun. Geese from the park make noises like cars. Cracks open up in London.

More tramps when the moon looks through. In Arlington House at the top of the hill more dossers and tramps (and neat failed people who keep to themselves so as not to look like tramps or dossers) sleep like bees in a beehive stack than anywhere else in London. Such narrow and acrid spaces. They try to keep them in order ... but the stories rustle and mutter, unravel as memory loosens. And Arlington House attracts to the gaps near the edge of the Park, where the moonlight streams, other tramps and dossers who do not live there but straggle and stain the respectable pavements. Some of them shift and stare all night as the slow stars move above them. *Keep us away from the daylight.* They shrink back into the darkness, move in the end to the public green in the fork of the roads which roar down to Euston, vague dusty green under fumes and thunder, and, dozing, hear only dazed bees humming, bees and no cars, drink cider and dream upon empty benches the dim fitful sounds of lost summer gardens, until they wake with a raging thirst in the blaze of day without water.

In Mornington Place the children who play in front of the houses see only the future: a shining immediate chapter where nothing runs out or away. Now they are stuck between winter and spring, but they know that summer will always come back, and the nearby trains will take them one day to wild green seas and the warm firm sands of tomorrow, where all they have wanted will be (*the taps, in fact, are about to run dry but tramps and children don't know that*).

Fat Mary rounded the Crescent in a creaking shell of paper. The paper was warm and light, although it was crusted with dirt. She had nearly changed it last week, then she thought of how spring was coming. In spring she would throw it away. By now it was like her skin. You grew into things that were close to you. For her there was only paper.

Fat Mary had not been a tramp for long, and she did not feel like the others. Whatever the others were like. Their drinking made them a mystery. In any case, ever since childhood she had always been told she was simple. Mary had never felt simple, but life had grown very long. And suddenly Mary saw they were right, her life was growing more simple.

It was since she had been a tramp, if a tramp was what she now was. Somebody yelled at her one day, 'Fuck off, gerout of here, dirty old tramp!' Till then she just thought life had changed. It might still have gone back to normal. Whatever *normal* once seemed: a bed and clocks and washing...

She had been outside one winter, and things would get better in spring.

Once she had needed so much, or believed that she needed so much. You needed things when you were young. To think she had once been young. The thought was so monumental, she stopped in her tracks to think it. Those little ones in the distance, sat in the sun on the doorstep. Was Mary ever so little, so limber? Some of the children liked her.

There was something Mary still needed. She stopped and stared at the girls. She needed to talk to people. It wasn't much, just to talk. She had so much to tell, and some of them liked her stories. She was fifty yards from the doorstep now and her mouth began to open.

'Fat Mary's a tramp,' said Kevin severely. He had seen her rooting in bins.

'No she isn't. She lives in a great big house in summer. She does, she told me,' said Anne.

'An' she went to the sea,' said Penny, her sister. 'She said it looked green, and she paddled. With fish.'

'Haddock,' Anne said. 'There. That proves it. You couldn't have tramps who went to the sea.'

'Well it's not summer now,' Kevin sneered at his neighbours. 'She *is* a tramp. An' she just tells stories.'

But he saw her coming, as broad as a whale, her grey mouth open, and he ran away.

The two little girls hadn't seen her yet, enclosed in their own short story. Locked in that square bright future chapter which might have chocolate, or not. Aunt Cindy might leave them some twenty pences, or else she was going to forget.

Gillian Reedy had told her daughters to *go outside and play*.

'Want to stay inside and play,' said Anne, not looking up from her book.

'Now get on and leave us in peace,' said Gill, holding out their coats. She was doing that grim quiet voice. 'I want to have a talk with Aunt Cindy.'

Cindy wasn't really their aunty, she was just an old school friend of Gill's. Anne was in love with Cindy though, who dressed like a magazine. Her hair was blonde and her clothes were blonde and she smelled of marzipan. Anne wouldn't argue in front of Cindy. She scowled and put her coat on.

'I need a man,' said Cindy, reflective, heavy-lidded eyes seeing nothing. (Cindy's life had gone wrong, Gill considered. She was still unmarried in her thirties.) But she didn't really sound depressed, not depressed enough to please Gillian. Too often she seemed to preen herself on the advantages of freedom. Sheathed in soft blonde wool (it had probably come from Jaeger), she looked too good to be true. Cindy never lost her temper.

'Well everyone *does* need a man,' Gill remarked as she closed the door. The two little voices miraculously ceased, and she said before she could help it, 'I sometimes think it's kids you don't need. Kids ... who needs them?'

'They're lovely kids,' said Cindy, shocked. 'Sometimes I don't understand you.'

They stared at each other, hard. Faintly, small quarrelling voices.

'I suppose they'll have to come in,' sighed Gill. Her anger with Cindy vanished. 'But it's lovely to be on our own. You need to be on your own.'

'I'm on my own all the time,' Cindy said. A chill gust rattled the window.

'They want a pet, that's the latest,' said Gill. 'A budgerigar, of all things.'

'Ahh,' said Cindy. 'Sweet. It's nice for kids to have pets.'

First they need heat, light, water. Then all the other small wants. Each small want breeds another small want so the net of needs is endless.

'It's all right for you,' said Gill, thin-lipped. 'But I'm not made of money. It's bad enough feeding the four of us without a menagerie.'

'Has he heard yet, by the way?' George Reedy was up for promotion. His wife had pushed him to try, though the job meant working away.

'Yes. He didn't get it, if you want to know. And we really needed the money.'

Anger was trying to burst the pane. Faintly, the little girls' voices: *were we ever as young as them?* Then Gillian heard Fat Mary.

Mary had got very close to the girls and her snaggled lips stretched wide. What she thought she was doing was smiling. She had so much to say. But the green door opened wider.

'Penny! Anne! Inside. It's time for elevenses.'

'Don't *wanter* come inside.'

'Penny! Do as you're told.'

Fat Mary was swinging her body round so she could address them all. Gill Reedy wouldn't meet her eyes. 'Come on,' she gritted to the girls.

'You'd be surprised how little you need.' Mary said. 'This is all I've got, what you see.'

But the small round listening faces were snatched away like money. One pale thin leg that had dangled behind was yanked back into the darkness. The green door slammed on its echo. The pale spring flowers trembled.

They trembled like lips, like flesh. She remembered when life had pale flesh. And clothes slipped away, warm hands, soft slopes. Now light lay flat on the step.

Once she had needed so much. Clean sheets, weekly baths, her wages. Her mother, who wrote every week; her lovers, of course; and love.

But life had started again, once she hadn't a bed to sleep in. At first it had just seemed chilly and lonely, but then she began to feel free. Her memories talked in the darkness. Lost loves swam towards focus. They went on forever, the trail of spilled beads, or balloons, perhaps, for their softness ... the faces, wavering – now clear, now muddy – then suddenly smiling and firm in the sunlight.

She still had her mother's photo, in a pale blue envelope. The photograph was a golden brown but she always saw it in colour. That was an interesting fact: you didn't need colour photos. It was one more useless invention, like cigarettes and bombs. As she looked at the photo, her mother's eyes blazed green and her hair was black. Nothing had changed since the day she died. Mary wished she had always known that.

All those years she had wasted being afraid of what she might lose. And then in the end she lost it all, and found her heart was still beating. You didn't die without washing, you didn't dry up without love.

But you did need someone to talk to. She wandered away from the step.

Inside the closed front door, the two girls sniffed in the hall. Anne had got a smacked leg for saying, 'You *told* us to go outside.' She was smacked for her 'tone of voice', and she cried for sheer unfairness.

'Well, this is cheerful,' said Cindy, staring at her beige suede bag. She shuffled her beige suede feet as if she were about to leave.

Gill was alarmed. 'You don't understand,' she appealed. 'You don't know what it's like. I get so tired with those kids.'

'Well I can see that,' said Cindy.

Gillian stiffened. (*Superior cow, sitting there showing off her Jaeger. I could buy Jaeger as well if I only had myself to look after.*) 'You know, I wouldn't change places,' she flushed, 'for all the tea in China.'

The sounds in the hall had changed: sniffs became quarrelling voices. 'How about a cuppa?' said Gillian suddenly, 'Sorry if I seem a bit sharp. It's my time of the month as well.' *(Why must I always say sorry?)*

Cindy gave half a smile, then the other half came to join it. 'That'd be nice,' she said. 'And shall we have one of those chocolates?'

Everyday life, ordinary life, everyday life in the city. But cities need heat, light, water for everyday life to go on.

Gillian went into her pale mauve kitchen to fill the electric kettle. The water gushed, then hesitated, slowed to a trickle, stopped. She crashed the kettle down in a fury, stupid steel against steel.

It couldn't have gone off here. They were right in the centre of town. You couldn't be left without water, right in the middle of the city.

She yanked the tap in a rage. A strangled sound, then nothing.

'Oh bloody Jesus, no.'

'They said it had come to London.'

The anger had come to London, the rage that cuts off the flow.

'We'll just have to have something cold,' said Cindy, with a meaningful glance at the sherry. 'Poor Gillian. How boring. But it probably won't last long.'

104

Mary remembered endless boredom when she used to live in houses. Some of the work she liked. The things where you saw the difference. Cleaning potatoes, or silver, making the white shine through. Some of the work was stupid though. Dusting: the dust came back. You could see the cloud of it hanging above you, waiting to settle in the sunlight. The dust motes danced and laughed, and the birds would be calling outside, and she would be trapped in her sweating body, waving rags out of windows: staying inside the glass, in the dusty, bullying houses.

And the high thin voices of her mistresses would screech out over the birdsong. 'If it's all the same with you, Walker, could you have your free evening tomorrow? Master has asked a few people round, and you might do something with the haddock.' *Hollandaise, Béarnaise, Mayonnaise.* 'Our cook has a talent for sauces.' But Mary wasn't a cook: she just did whatever was wanted. Days and days of her life had slipped by, sucked down in slippery sauces. There was pleasure in making rich thick liquids, velvety things, the oil in slow droplets, making it fall as patient as rain, but all that came back was smeared dishes.

Running the water to wash them up, she never knew it was there. It was always too hot or too cold, and it simply went with the houses.

'I'm sure that it won't last long,' Cindy said again, seeing the girls' scared faces. Anne was pulling at her mother's arm. A packet of biscuits went flying.

'NOW SEE WHAT YOU'VE DONE,' Gill screamed. 'Every single one will be broken! Do you think we're made of money?'

The silence that followed was terrific, with a single drip from the tap. Plop on the steel, then nothing. Gill turned to the wall, ashamed.

'There's George might go for interviews and he won't be able to bath. And how can I cook the dinner tonight if I haven't got any water?'

Normal, everyday life, everyday life in the city. But now the water main's burst and flooded and nothing is quite so normal.

Gillian's mouth was clenched and strange. 'We're going to have a sherry. And a plate of sodding biscuits.' She slopped out two large sherries.

The two little girls sat quietly munching and listened to Mum and Aunt Cindy. They were talking about peculiar things, the thing called *sex,* and men. It was men who did the sex, and most of them sounded horrid. Dad was another kind of man, they supposed. But Mum was pretending not to like him. He wasn't any good at his job, he hadn't any 'get up and go'. Which was why they were living in England. Moreover, England was finished. Mum wouldn't take it sitting down. She had sent him off to the library. He was looking for jobs in the papers. Well, was he a man or a mouse?

Cindy on the other hand wanted a man 'to be father to her children'. And this was surprising to Penny and Anne who thought Cindy hadn't got children.

Mum had gone pink all over and suddenly got very happy. She giggled a lot and made silly jokes and her hair had come down in strands. She filled up their glasses three times, and her daughters ate all the biscuits. She noticed but she didn't get cross. 'It's your fault if your Mum gets tipsy,' she said and she pointed at them, but crooked, and laughed, and her words were blurry.

Later the sherry would take its revenge by making their Mum very thirsty.

Mary had found that she needed water as soon as she started to live outside. Until you had gone outside for good and away from the endless taps and basins and sinks and showers and baths and cisterns, you didn't know what you needed.

Out in the street they were working their mouths in desire for just a dribble. Something to rinse their salty lips after sucking chicken bones left in bins. 'Thirsty,' they moaned in the early hours, as last night's cider shrivelled their throats, 'thirsty,' they sighed as their dry thick tongues strained back at the fur in their gullets.

So Mary giggled and shivered and smiled to see the lake on Mornington Crescent. To her it was something miraculous. Water set free for the tramps. She watched the workmen benignly, humming and rubbing her hands. A tall pipe grew like a sapling tree with two generous spouts of brass.

When the workmen finished she thanked them. 'It's not just for *you*, Missis.' They were young and laughing and nervous. They didn't expect any thank yous. A stupid old gaffer had threatened them, blustered about the war. And this old woman was worse, in a way. Slobbering, gave you the creeps.

She stood and smiled at the standpipe, the magic tree of brass. There was water whenever she wanted it now, no problem getting through green locked doors, no problem creasing your face in two, crawling to barmaids or waiters.

And the magic worked on them all: it would bring all the strangers out of their houses, draw all the faces back her way, melt the glass and the curtains.

Now they were all in the dark together, queueing in the cold at night. And the pipes led down to the heart of things, to the wilderness of lost water.

All of them had to learn quickly, and all that they learned was bad. How often they wanted to wash their hands, now that they couldn't do it. How fast the dirty underwear piled, how sinks and baths grew grey. How long and cold a queue can become when you all want water for breakfast. How quickly a lavatory starts to smell when you only flush it with buckets.

'People might die,' Gill Reedy huffed, meeting Mr Goff on the corner.

'Bloody disgrace,' he grunted. 'In the last war folks had some spirit. In those days, Madam, these water-worker Johnnies would have been shot on the spot.'

Gillian fumed at her husband in bed. 'England is going to the dogs,' she said. 'Now we haven't even got water. Nobody's got any guts –' (George knew his wife meant him. His teeth were coated with acid) '– We ought to go and start afresh. In Australia or somewhere. You would if you were a man. You know that I'm behind you.'

With that she curled up and went to sleep and he lay awake and wretched.

Next day George came back from the office with something to please his wife.

'You remember I once learned Spanish,' he said, very timid, at tea. 'There's something in South America, in charge of the office out there. I'd be earning three times as much money. There are snakes and things, I suppose –'

'I'll think about it,' Gill said. Later she thought, and smiled. Gold, and humming-birds, tanned explorers, and well-insured husbands, and snakes. However, the very same day she found this fact in *The Mirror.*

'*Did you know ... ?* In Calama in Chile there is no record of rain ever falling.'

She wanted to be quite sure. That night in bed she asked him. 'Is Chile in South America?'

'Of course,' he said, half-asleep.

She didn't like that smug '*of course*' but for once she let it pass.

'I don't think you ought to take that job after all,' she told his back, very firmly. 'Money's not everything, George, you know.' Next day she threw out the paper.

Fat Mary would fish it out of the bin: Fat Mary would read her stars: it said that Pisces was wise that day. So perhaps she was not so simple.

Fat Mary had felt her wisdom since the water strike came to the city. You don't need much, she thought. But everybody needs water.

Water became transparent again after one week bright as blood. The water-workers went back to work, and took the brass trees with them. Embarrassing needs slid back underground, the city veiled its entrails. Water belonged to the rich again, and tramps and dossers went thirsty. Baths ran deep as before, the sleepy pink bodies floated.

Fat Mary died in September, escaping another winter. She didn't need very much, it was true, but a little more would have helped.

She knew that she needed heat, wrapping herself in paper. She knew that she needed light, with those frightening feet in the dark. She knew that she needed water, laughing to see the stand-pipe, laughing with joy to see the glittering lake leak over the Crescent.

But so many people walked past her.

'Talks to herself,' they said.

I was talking to you, my dears, she said to herself as she died.

Mornington children were sad for a bit when Mary disappeared.

'Fat Mary's dead, Fat Mary's dead.'

They enjoyed being sad in autumn.

Little Penny made herself cry, sitting on the chilly step.

'She wasn't a tramp,' she screamed at Kevin. 'She told me about the sea.'

'Penny! Come in and have your bath!' her mother called from inside the house, but Penny sat on and talked to the moon. It was round and white, and its mouth was open. It didn't seem very far away.

'Hallo, Mary. Come back soon.'

Beautiful Things

They never said thank you for the presents.

Which were beautiful, weren't they? Beautiful things. Expensive. Every time Jane stared at her still white face in the mirror, unhappy, now, unadorned, the face of her family, she thought of her sister's kids and the presents.

She had stopped herself ringing many times. It's different for her, Jane told herself. Working. Two kids. She's just busy.

All the same, she needed some word, some return.

What had she given them? Books, children's classics in handsome gift editions, things that the kids would grow into one day, a new world, she had thought when she bought them, something to take her nephews away from the telly that flickered against the daylight from morning till night. She had bundled her purse out of her bag as fast as she could to show she had money, comforting thick new glossy wads of money the equal of anyone else's, proving that she was a person, someone with a right to touch the tooled leather of the books, not someone abandoned, a widow, half what she was.

Yet she did feel so reduced. They had drawn her, the shops,

since she had been widowed, shining in the distance, offering a welcome to the lonely, though on the way home she ached. Big stores like vast overheated lagoons where she could sail on the effortless escalators up to Furniture and Fittings, looking at new cream velvety carpets now there was no danger from Kingsley's dropped ash, picking up china figurines of neat miniature people to live with her in the silence, beautiful things to take home. It was always a long way home.

Sometimes at night, since her husband had died, Jane felt that her life was a minuscule capsule of light and safety surrounded by thousands of miles of cold gleaming streets and unfriendly pavements and sudden terrifying movements of hungry living things. Then again, sometimes the safety of the hot lit house was too much and she longed for fresh air, longed for someone, anyone, to phone or write to or dance with in the street, or dive in through the window and claim a kiss as easily as Kingsley once kissed her, coming home: 'Mmm. Is it chicken? I can smell garlic. Thanks, my love.'

But to widows, nothing happens. No reason for a chicken to sizzle in the pan, no plantain frying.

Christmas was a time of false hope. Tearing open her cards, which said 'Thinking of you', 'Take care of yourself' (because *they* didn't care), 'Come and see us!' (but never a time or place), 'Hope you're managing okay' (as if she had a business), 'Best love' – but if they loved her best, why did no one ever visit?

She'd spent Christmas Day with Kingsley's family, who welcomed her, sadly, going to the Pentecostal Church with them, though it wasn't her church and hadn't been Kingsley's for over a decade. Missing Kingsley so much, she had come home too soon, driving back to her empty house with the lights left on against thieves and the battlements of beautiful, silent things she had bought with the life insurance and the university pension which Kingsley had only told her to expect when he was almost dead of lung cancer.

New Year tasted bitter. The weeks crawled by. *They never said thank you* ... Forget it, let go. She drove herself out of the house, out into the back garden where she hardly ever went these days, wrenching back the bolts, chains, stupidly frustrating armoury of locks and unfindable keys that the police recommended for women alone. Strong as death, the back door, but she was stronger.

Her garden was dank and sparse with early February, one of a double row between mean streets that she'd never thought of as mean when she lived here with Kingsley. Then, every room in the house had been scattered with books and papers, his writing, their food, which he loved, his ashtrays, grey, overflowing: temporary things not permanent things, shed feathers and fur of two beings living over and under and inside each other, for they were very happy, still very much lovers when she first began to notice his cough wasn't going away and he was too thin. They used to dance, laugh, fly.

Now the house was different, immaculate. Nearly every week since the money had arrived she had bought something new that Kingsley might have liked, to make it a little more perfect: a cushion, a bowl, a bookcase, two chairs, a vase. And felt more afraid. For it must be dangerous to have such beautiful things. Which the world would try to take from her, as Kingsley was taken away.

Hardly any light in the garden. Why weren't there any snowdrops this year? Staring down, Jane noticed a bulb, upturned, naked, white and shiny, lying on the black soil, a green curved funnel of leaf sailing stoutly off to one side. Uprooted by something, but not dead yet. Then she saw another. What?

Right beside her, noiseless, at her feet, glistening, stalled in the middle of a zigzag motion, quivering minutely, watching her with bright black button eyes, alive: a grey squirrel. Now one step nearer, front paws pressed flat on the ground, head cocked.

She bent to press the bulbs back in, slowly so as not to alarm him, but he fled up the apple tree and over the fence in a series of graceful, weightless leaps, *come back!* He was gone.

And the uprooted bulbs might die. Everything got lost, taken, stolen.

A little rush of lonely indignation sent her straight inside to the phone. She would ring Sheilah now, *why not?* Dialling her sister's number with rigid fingers.

'Hallo?' Her sister's familiar flat voice.

'Did you get the presents all right?'

'Yes.'

'Did you like them?'

A pause. 'You shouldn't have, Jane. Such beautiful things.'

A real note of complaint. As if they didn't deserve them, Jane thought. Perhaps she's right.

'So they did arrive then,' she said, with cool unkindness.

'Of course they arrived. You're saying the kids should have written, aren't you?'

The doorbell detonated, violently loud, two feet from where Jane stood gripping the phone in the hall, and her heart jerked and leaped.

'It's the door –'

'I'm not deaf –'

The bell stopped, then another great blare of sound, then another. '*Wait!*' she yelled at the door, then to Sheilah, 'Hang on for a moment,' glad to bang the receiver down on its side on the hall table.

The man stood on the doorstep, too close to the door so she almost fell over him, a small man, grinning, twitching, flinging open his hands in welcome, tight silver-grey curls as he bobbed his head, blinked his dark eyes. Unfamiliar, surely. But he seemed to know her. 'We-ell,' he said, 'where's my man, my good friend?'

'Who –?'

'Your husband, my friend. I need a little bit of help,' conspiratorially, bowing and touching his forehead, then off on his story before she could take a deep breath and tell him that Kingsley was dead. 'I live jus' down the road, you know, three, four doors away. We got the old-fashioned toilet, you know, and the cistern it's gone and come right off the wall, the water gone through the ceiling and wreckin' the carpets, you never see such a mess, and I think of my friend and I think him gwaan lend me ten pound so I can go to the plumber shop and get me a ballcock, give it you straight back.'

'Yes,' she said dumbly, 'of course, I could lend you –' Then stopped. Because she knew all her neighbours, didn't she? Didn't forget faces. I don't know you, she thought, and you never knew Kingsley, did you? You're a con man, a brilliant con man –

But was he? For there was a plumber's shop on the corner, though there was a betting shop too – and how could he know she had a husband? Nonsense. He guessed.

But if he's really a neighbour, and water's pouring through his ceiling –

'He's dead, my husband,' she said. 'Didn't you know he was dead? If you were his friend –'

'That's terrible, terrible,' he said, but impatiently, contorting his frame more and more, bending forward and back again, rocking, the low wintry sun springing over his crest of frosted grey curls, 'so him dead, him gone, rest his soul ... I need jus' ten pounds, for a few hours is all, you get it back when the wife comes home, no problem. Right?'

Then she said: 'I'll come with you to the plumber's, that's best.' Because she would not be made a fool of, stolen from, left with nothing, unthanked, abandoned.

'No, no, that's all right.' He was dipping and diving, hopping from foot to foot in her doorway, ready to run, dance, lie, fly, win horse races, interrupt phone calls, dive through the door and take all her money and never never thank her ...

She suddenly saw he might save her.

Then the phone began to squeak, repetitive, petty, a small pallid whine. *No.* Jane ignored it. Sifting through the ten-pound notes in her bag, thin pigeon-coloured things, just one from so many, of course she could afford it. 'Take it.' He grasped it in an instant, was turning away –

She knew if she jumped on his shoulders he'd run down the road with her like an athlete, nip into the betting shop, treble their money by shuffling it up into storm clouds of racing pigeons, straight out through the back and away into the beckoning streets beyond, away down the great noisy arteries and veins of blue roads and alleys and pathways forking and budding and forking again as the weather grows warmer and sky begins to leak between the tiles and pour around the sides of the tower blocks, pale blue, brighter blue, sun like a slow flash of lightning washing through walls and opening windows and now they are riding a widening river of light away into spring –

And the doors of the house are left open for squirrels to enter, so the beautiful things will be stolen, one after another, pale porcelain figures perched in the apple trees a little while longer before they crash down, her carpets pecked at for birds nests, her mirror a multi-coloured jigsaw of bluebells, daffodils, tulips.

And the phone moans on at blue air, which blows through, and lets go, and forgets.

What Was Important

As Cecily tried to get her trolley, two old men stood full in the way, talking explosively in Arabic, waving their hands, too loud for London. Probably the war, Cecily considered, but she spoke as clearly as she could, and smiled. 'Coming through, sorry,' she carolled. 'Terribly sorry, I have a family to feed.' Once she grasped her trolley, the polite smile died.

The supermarket felt big and unhelpful, chilled as death, indifferent, full of the wrong kind of packaged meat, steaming with ice as she poked and shivered. She was alone, and the young were leaving. Did her husband love her? He never said. If Gabriel loved her, she would be all right. Cecily told herself that she knew what was important.

Today, though, had gone wrong from the beginning. She had been busy for days, tidying and shopping, getting things ready for the big party, but still life managed to trip you up: all those tangles of littleness. Cecily had quarrelled mildly with Pam, annoyed Gabriel by asking him to come home early, failed to clinch a time with the emergency plumber for the lavatory (now that *was* important! on a day when she was entertaining twenty people!)

then twice missed phone calls that might have been him. Oh, and last night when they were coming through the door the phone stopped just as she reached it. The second time the bell shrilled today she was suddenly shot with adrenalin, frantic, scrabbling up from hands and knees where she had been weeding, out in the cold, some mad voice saying *It's life and death!* She still just failed to get there in time.

And then she had seen it was gone two o'clock. So yet again, when she should have rung back, Cecily had dashed out to the shops, or they would have run out of the right kind of chicken, and the day would have turned into total disaster. *I just hope none of the guests has diarrhoea.* On the car radio there was news of war, but Iraqi place-names meant little to her.

The fridge was a blaze of photographic light. Inside she could see only whole pale bodies. Exasperated, Cecily beckoned over a stolid young Muslim in a headscarf. 'Where are the thighs?' she demanded, crossly. 'Where are the wings? You always have wings.'

'Cooked or raw?' The girl said, unsmiling.

'Cooked, of course,' she snapped, unfairly, and felt guilty to see the plain face flinch, under its frowning band of cloth. To compensate, she started babbling. 'For a barbecue, sorry. You couldn't know. Nice cooked joints for a barbecue.'

'Did you say *cooked*? For a barbecue?' Now the creature sneered, as if she was unbalanced. Cecily wasn't going to explain to her that this was an autumn barbecue, that most of the food would be warmed in the oven and just finished off outside on the fire.

'Look over there then,' the child instructed, with a face that said some people were beyond helping. Cecily did not thank her, though she found what she wanted, honey-gold limbs of corn-fed birds, ranked in pairs, ready-cooked, glistening, slicked with oil and flamed at the edges. And some nice-looking steaks (men did like meat). Cut very thin so it would cook quickly. She rushed on round the store, swooping on sausages, mushrooms, salad, barbecue buns, expensive wine to cheer up the adults, the usual sugary drinks for the twins. Then she remembered: they were adults too. She put back the cans and clanked in more wine.

They were growing up. They were going away. The barbecue was to mark the moment. Sam and Pam. They were not identical, had never been dressed in matching clothes, but now they were heading for the same frontier. And they were all leaving, all the young, flitting like swallows to their brave new world, except the spoiled ones who were having a gap year. She had asked round a dozen or so of their friends, all of them going to different universities, and their parents too, to celebrate.

There was nothing to be sad about, nothing at all. This was a new stage, a new beginning. Cecily and Gabriel, alone together. On the way to the till, she snatched up a paper. On the front page, the wretched war, a black and white picture of flames and confusion. Words were written across the photo. She glanced at it briefly. Must be some kind of poster. This particular tabloid was not pro-war. Without her glasses she couldn't really see. Thank heavens it would soon be over. She had a nephew, David, in the army.

A boy was standing near the newspaper stand, gangling, tall, surely younger than twenty, but with a full beard and the little round hat that said 'Muslim extremist' to her. He seemed to be watching her with interest. Some of the twins' friends were Muslim – or was it Hindu? She had asked many times, but always forgot. He had a biro behind his ear. Not much older than the twins, she thought, and gave him a liberal, accepting smile. He seemed to snicker, and turn away.

The traffic was appalling. Her life was hard. She sat there, knuckles white on the wheel, and suddenly noticed, and tried to calm down. 'Count your blessings,' she told herself. Her family was surely a blessing. In the end, family was the thing that mattered.

Sam was a sweetie. He had done so well. Samuel had never let them down. Pam had always been difficult, beautiful, maybe, but all over the place, rash and wilful, getting into trouble. She should have been the boy, they had always said. Muscular, tall, with that thick yellow hair which sprang from her head like a waterfall. Sam, by contrast, was quiet and brainy, frighteningly quick at science and maths, what the other children called a 'boffin'. A kind boy, sensitive, rather fat. It wasn't true that her son annoyed her. Pam was a daddy's girl, of course. The two of them were inseparable. 'Well now they'll be separated,' she thought, and was ashamed to feel a small thrill of triumph. Now she would have Gabriel all to herself.

But would she be enough for him? She had never been quite sure that she mattered to her husband. Other people's men were more demonstrative. Other wives were, well, luckier. When she asked him if he loved her, he just said 'Of course.' The words didn't come to him, that was all.

'Is anyone going to help?' she called, as she staggered in to the house with her bags. 'Pam! PAM! ... Sam ... are you there?'

It was Sam, of course, who came and helped, well-meaning but inept, as usual, managing to drop half the grapes on the floor ('We could tread them,' he said, trying to be cheerful). She sighed as she peeled the squashed skins from the tiles, pale as frog-spawn; the same old Sam.

'I'll do that, Mum.'

'It's all right. I've got a headache.'

He made her go upstairs for a rest and brought her up some tea, and a biscuit sodden with the liquid slopped in the saucer.

Still, she had a moment of pure pleasure as she tucked her aching feet up on the bed and reached across for the newspaper. Today was the 'Health' day, which she always enjoyed, noting every new herb and potion, planning ways to improve the condition of the troops, for Sam was shockingly soft and unfit (Pam was the one who did weight-lifting) and Gabriel, of course, was two stone too heavy, as she last remarked last night, at table: 'Your father is *dreadfully* overweight.' 'Don't say it in front of me, though,' said Gabriel. Middle-aged men did tend to be touchy.

Lean men. Beautiful, hard male bodies. She found herself thinking of her nephew David as she leafed through the pages of diet advice, the stories of death during liposuction, 'My stomach staples left me in a coma.' David, the son of her husband's brother, was effortlessly tall and fit, sleek and golden, graceful, male, needing to shave twice a day, when he lived with them, to keep his cheeks smooth, and there was always that sexy blue shadow. Not that she fancied him, of course. She was far too sensible to fancy her nephew. She had known him since he was a tiny child, when he used to run rings around Sam at football. But fondness, affection, a *tendresse* – she was not ashamed of feeling that. (What was the truth? *He was her favourite*. In some ways, he looked like a younger Gabriel. And Gabriel adored him, uncritically. Odd when he was quite hard on Sam.)

For two years David had been under their roof, after he quarrelled with his father, finishing his sixth form *en famille* with them. He was their second son, really, or so she told him, hoping that Sam wasn't listening. David was never a swot like Sam. He had so many friends, such fun, such charm. The house was alive when David was there. In her memory, Cecily was always laughing then, though David was erratic, noisy, moody. But of course when the exam results came through, his parents made David feel so guilty that he went off to redeem himself in the army ('It's going to be brilliant – adventure, travel, and Dad will finally be proud of me.' 'But David', she'd said, 'there is a war on.' 'Oh come on, Aunty, we'll have a laugh. Don't worry about it. I'll send you a postcard.') And now, bizarrely, he was in Iraq, but she supposed he was an officer, surely? Or maybe not, with grades like those. In any case, soon he would buy himself out. None of the family had ever been soldiers.

Had David written? Of course he hadn't (whereas Sam had promised he would text her every day when he got to university, and she was forced to suppress irritation. 'No, my darling, you'll be too busy,' she had said, kindly, but Sam looked back, owlish, and said, with patent sincerity, 'I could never be too busy for my mother.').

She told herself to go down and start cooking, but glanced, in parting, at the paper's front page. At first she stared, uncomprehending, but then she realised that the writing across it was not, in fact, part of the picture at all. Someone had scribbled on her paper. A biro addition by some stranger. The photograph was black-and-white, of a tank with a ragged crown of flames, somewhere in Iraq, she deduced. A hot white sky, a mess of burning. The letters, not well-formed, sprawling, asked 'WHAT HE THINK, THIS IS HOLIDAY SO HE GET SUN-TAN?'

She took a second look at the photo and realised she had completely failed to see the blazing figure at its centre, leaping from the tank, a burning man, fringed with fire down his straight narrow outline like a mane of flame on a horse's neck, but when she looked closer the fire was eating him, small savage tooth-marks eroding his outline. 'WHAT HE THINK ... HE GET SUN-TAN?'

Burning to death. What would that be like? She thought of it with crawling horror, the uniform melting, sticking to you –

'Mum, the loo still isn't flushing!'

'Coming,' she said, and put the paper aside after a long last look at the scrawled graffiti. Some angry Muslim must have done it. Perhaps the young man by the supermarket till. She thought with irritation of his bushy beard. Thank God David would be home for Christmas. She went to the bathroom to wash her hands, feeling the paper was contaminating.

Sam was standing on the loo seat, perched awkwardly, his little round gut straining up over his jeans, trying to peer into the high cistern that had been there when they first moved to the house – somehow, Gabriel had never replaced it (but the children had grown up; all those years had gone).

'Get down Sam, you'll never manage it.' She could not control an edge of impatience, and he thundered down, grunting, flinging out one arm, which managed to knock over the blue-striped toothbrush mug, scattering the tight little family of toothbrushes which flew across the floor as the china shattered.

'Honestly Sam, leave it alone ... I'm going to have to get the man.'

'*I am a man*,' he said, rattled. 'I can do things, Mum. Give me a chance.'

'*The* man, I said. I meant the plumber. Oh, please, Sam, do stop fussing with that!' (For now he was sprawling on the floor at her feet, scrabbling after the toothbrushes, his large soft bottom right under her nose.) But his eyes were so hurt behind his glasses that she felt ashamed, and resolved to do better.

Quite soon she was hacking at the steaks while Sam mooned about in the kitchen doorway. She only wanted them all to be happy. 'By the way, Sam, is Rafiq coming? Is he still vegetarian?'

'Yes, Rafiq, and both his parents, but it isn't Rafiq's lot who are veggie. It's Fadia actually. She's become a vegan.'

'Muslims are a bit difficult, aren't they?'

'It's nothing to do with being a Muslim. She'll eat the rice and the barbecue buns.'

'She can have extra wine,' said Cecily, kindly, and then remembered – 'No, they don't drink. Well, I've got lots of coke and things.'

'Fadia could drink you under the table.'

His knowing, superior face annoyed her. 'They're not best at *everything*, you know. Why don't you go and get the barbie ready? It's supposed to be a boys' thing, doing the fire, and your father won't be back until seven.'

'I'm doing it, Ma, I've fixed it with Dad,' Pam yelled through, over the noise of the TV. Both children were deaf unless they wanted to hear. 'Dad's said he wants *me* to do it with him. I'm brilliant with fires. I'm about to get started.'

'You're to let your brother have a go,' snapped Cecily. 'It isn't fair to leave him out.'

'I'm not a child,' Sam said, mildly.

'All right then Sambo, follow me,' said Pam, hoving through into the kitchen, shouldering him sideways as she did so. 'But you can't make a fire in those teddy-bear slippers.'

'Can I do the salad?' Sam asked his mother, who was slicing the fat off the scarlet muscle. There was more gristle than she expected. She cut too hard and sliced her thumb. That was it: disaster when you least expected it. Blood flowered red on the kitchen towel. 'No,' she exploded. 'Just go away, Sam.'

'I will soon be gone,' he said, with dignity. 'Remember, that's why you're having this party.'

'Don't be a bitch, Mum,' Pam said, lightly, hugging her brother as she pushed out of the door, her thick hair bright, impenetrable. 'He's probably capable of cutting up a lettuce.'

Cecily caught her arm, on a sudden impulse, and turned to

Sam, and clutched his hand. 'I love you both.' They stood like statues in the hard kitchen light, then the twins both laughed and Sam ruffled her hair. 'All right Mum. *Eee*-asy now.'

Her husband was late. Most of the guests were here: the garden was filling up with noise and laughter, a pool of warm sound in the gathering cold. 'Bring out some water,' Sam called to Pam, who was carrying a jug of punch from the kitchen, and she shook her head and smiled at him. 'Sam, it's a party, people don't need water.' The sky was the deep glowing blue after sunset, a band of lemon-gold around the urban horizon sharpening the scarce-leaved trees and the rooftops. Silver planes scored slowly across from Heathrow, people flying off into the hopeful evening, and the children would fly, she thought, all over the world, who knew where they would go, but *make them safe and happy*. She herself was happy, now, suddenly. Her white pyrocanthus, so lovely this year, had a depth like lit bone against the indigo, everything was perfect, perfectly peaceful: how silly to have let that paper upset her. The birds fell quiet; the barbecue glowed, red-and-white coals at the top of the lawn, and the young people's bodies flashed smoothly past the fire as they wheeled and gyrated and greeted each other, hugging as if they could never part, long hair flickering out like water, the fire silhouetting their strong young limbs, their heads made heroic by haloes of flame, and briefly there was an outburst of screams as a spark caught Pam's great hanks of blonde hair but was stifled at once by Sam with his jumper – 'Get OFF Sam, stop being a dickhead' – leaving them louder and merrier. All of them are here, thought Cecily, moved – Rafiq and Emily, Bunny with

Adam, both the Fosters, oh, and there's Fadia, Simeon with Nina, Bessie and Musa, the Caldecott clan and Leonie and Sarah and, just for once, it seemed, all the fathers ... She relaxed at last as she saw, in the distance, her own husband pushing out through the glass doors, as if in slow motion, it seemed to her, compared to the fluid bodies of the children, and she sucked her first long cold drink of champagne and savoured the salt-and-sweet smell of meat cooking. *All of us are here in this garden together. As if we shall never change or die. All of the faces from my children's childhood. They have grown up. Thank God, we have made it.*

And the flushed, roughened faces of the other parents smiled as she called 'At last, here's Gabriel. Now, a toast to all our children!'

But why is he walking so slowly, so heavily? The phone in the house is ringing again and as Gabriel comes nearer, people fall away, and he says 'My ldear love, it's about David –'

Into the Blue

In, in, out of the noise and glare! That white cold light of London, which I have only known since passing over. Now flitting through the world like a shadowless sparrow, I see them all, I know them all, these many lands I never saw nor painted.

No more painting now, no lovely limbs, no cunning hands to shape the world. I thought that it would last forever once. No matter. No complaints.

I had her once, I held her once. I captured her. All of us think these things will last forever.

As do the rushing forms all round me. Jostling into the museum out of the busy daylight, clutching their money, pulling along their young, their darling future, pressing their faces blindly against the present, even as it softens and crumbles away. Children who will be old in a blink, in the silver crossing of one small cloud. How long ago my own children fell into dust, over four hundred years now. A breath on the great slow skin of the ocean.

My children. And her children.

(They too had children, skipping away ...)

Some things stay with me forever, though. Her pale tender face.
Her eyes like pools of still black water. Black and bright. So
accursed bright. In them, small sharp-cut windows of light. And
her lips, haunting me like a wine stain. Some things I did get right.
I think I did – they said I did. For her portrait, ravishing, ruffed
with fur, rough thick cream with sweet tippets of dark pushing
out like petals round her slender waist, her springy black hair
only half-hidden, pulled casually back with a veil like a cloud, its
edgelet frilled like the lips of a shell – I had, for once, my meed of
praise. The crowds gathered to look her over, they all knew her,
they thought they did, the beautiful Jewess who lived on the hill,
though few of them knew – none of them knew what the two of
us knew –

I promised never to destroy her. I could not give her what
Greco did, with his lying brushes dipped in gold. Whatever he
did, it turned to money. He took care of her, though they never
married.

I caught her beauty, though. In the flash of the moment when
it lived and glowed. Which means she has never left me. Can
never escape me, even if –

On, on, left hand down, kick the right leg, make a swift corner
... Effortless travel is a benefit. As I think, I turn: one look, and
I swoop. Transparent angels, we throng the air. If those below
only knew we were here ... They still would not know us, for no
one knows us. That is my sentence: loneliness. As a restless soul,
I must wander forever, never dissolve into blue air. Grudge and
hunger: they keep me going. And once the Greek was in torment

too. For centuries, he was a lost soul like me, his pieces kept in damp churches, forgotten.

In, in to the palace of art. We had palaces too, though those long-nosed Habsburgs never liked my work enough. Never saw what we Toledans had, and I could not take my chance in Madrid ... To succeed, I should have gone to Madrid. I could not leave her, was the truth of it. Besides, I was no trimmer, no greaser, no bower and smiler as he must have been. The Greek, the lucky one, El Griego. Now called by the bastard name El Greco, something of nothing, half and half, 'Le Greco' to those dogs the French. All the time, he swore he was a Cretan –

His charmed, damned, footling life, the life that made him rich as Midas, though he squabbled with the kings, rowed with the priests, demanded more money, committed heresies, claimed he could outpaint Michelangelo. They all forgave him. They flocked around him. He came to Toledo and stole my thunder. Why couldn't the villain have stayed in Madrid? Bad behaviour made him famous. Then he stole her, and I watched him do it. He gave her what I could not give.

My earthly life lasted longer than his. The sweet satisfaction of seeing him buried, although it was in the high cathedral. Then still more honey: the son, poor bastard, poor Jorge Manuel with his great haunted orbs, soon could not pay the rent for the plot, for the money ran out, my love had run through it, and Jorge was gifted but impractical. The Greek's bones were dragged out and carted off, still with the rags of flesh upon them. Re-interred in a cheaper spot. I laughed, I crowed to hear the news. By the time I died, we were both equally forgotten. And for nearly two centuries we hung out together, disgruntled angels still longing for fame, travelling the earth when our names were whispered, too often getting there to find we were deluded, some starveling nonentity had borrowed our syllables ...

But then Greco's name came back. Floated up into the sunlight from the bottom of the pond. Horror: his golden afterlife, the torment of his resurrection. Watching my rival, once obscure as me, start to shine in the light of posthumous praise. Three centuries later, how could I expect it! Hearing fools claim he was not awkward, but bold! Not hysterical, but a *mannerist*! Not a clumsy colorist, but an innovator! Acid pinks, crude blues, shrieking greens ... The dense oily blackness of his *disegno*! Now he's claimed as the forerunner of all these clowns, the modern painters who daub like apes. I wonder if it makes him happy. He burned for fame more than any of them (Not more than me. I burned. Still burn.).

Those new cubist madmen drew freaks like his, human beings who had been stretched on the wrack, everything wrenched out of harmony. The poltroon Cézanne with his monkish beard ... now Greco is all the rage again, every feeble art student knows his name, blazoned on a banner outside this gallery, shouting his folly across the broad square, huge as a fabled elephant or camel, farting out *Greck, Greck, Greck*.

Not that I care. No, it's all gone. Just a brief blaze-up of the old passion. Leave it behind.

In, in.

This gallery's a miracle of science. It has engines, which raise up the old and the fat (so many of them portly, so many of them old, in my day all the people were lean and young, and died that way, still black-haired and hungry – angry, I suppose I died angry – what is this new race of pale, bloated men?). And those buzzing boxes that take in money and disgorge tokens for the hoi polloi – I have no truck with them, I am an artist, one of death's new aristocrats, elegant, weightless, lacking coarse flesh. I march in boldly past the slave taking tickets.

Yes, yes, Greco's usual extravagant stuff. I need not pause long to look at it, though some strange voice inside me whispers 'stay', for just once or twice, a window has opened, I have looked at his paintings and seen miracles. I have seen through into the blue blue air, the electric skies where he perhaps has – yes. The skies where he has genius.

But his figures were always deformed, inhuman, tall as church spires or cypresses. And white as lead, white as death. He killed the subjects of his portraits. Stretching them out, depleting them. He said he liked *colore* more than *disegno* – trilling out the terms to show he'd been to Venice! – yet that livid white is what I see as his colour, the unreal pallor of chalk or clay, paint like the deathly light of London. No wonder this city honours him. Now the English cluster and push around him, peering at his cursed canvases, these modern-day giants, so fat, so tall, smelling of hideous chemicals, chattering and grinning and shoving like servants. Purify the temple! Throw them all out! Leave me, at last, on my own with him.

I will lie here and wait, since I cannot sleep. I have not slept for three hundred years. Sometimes I fall into a swoon like a stone into the ocean, or I dream of the past with my eyes open, but the gentle loosening of sleep is denied us. Real human sleep, its soft unravelling, is not for spectres, for if we lose our grip, we dissolve into the void and are lost for ever, though often and often I have longed for that … But no, I will lie here, harming no one. They may tread upon me, they may step through me, for I am no impediment. I am impotent, but I was potent once –

Yes, sink down here on this low hard seat, and they may all sit on top of me, my bones are of crystal, my bones are air, I stretch myself out in the net of warm voices …

And I am in Toledo again. In Toledo, and in her arms. Her white silk skin, her raspberry breasts, the way she laughed softly and let me in. Her nether fur where I sucked and burrowed. He stole her away, but never entirely. Under his nose we went at it like monkeys … at it like angels, sometimes, too. Fledged with laughter and tenderness. On breezy summer afternoons. When the warm winds blew across to Toledo. Her house on the hill. Her flesh-coloured walls, her small room, dark, scented with orient spice, cinnamon and ginger from paradise. Maybe that's how she ran through his money, for spices were luxuries when we were young, in that bright morning, far away. She was my love, and I was hers. Not just the act like the beasts in the field. Look back in wonder at what I had, the easy perfection I took for granted, the happy body which lay close to hers. On her, in her. Our May, our June. The young never see how miraculous.

It's night-time now, and the lights still blaze, but the hideous living have all gone home. Now I can stroll and sneer at my leisure.

He is good, that's the trouble. Mad, but good. Demented, cross-eyed, sometimes cack-handed. Something there, though. That shivering thing. That moment when the hair stands on end. He couldn't catch life, but he made a world. A weird world that never existed. Long-limbed, spectral-faced, shadowy beings, colours shrieking like acid fruit, heavens writhing with snake-limbed saints ...

Did he ever manage to paint a real person? What was quick and warm escaped him, always. First you have to feel for them. Did he feel for her? Could he feel for the boy? That gentle boy with thoughtful eyes, building his wooden towers after lessons. Even the child had to be changed, stolen, painted in that great pompous piece, the *Burial of the Conde de Orgaz*, his grave small face at the very front, his two great eyes, always older than his years, and in his pocket, that piece of paper saying '*Greco fecit*' – Greco made me. *Greco made me*, so the fool boasted, and because he painted it, it becomes true. Nothing was real for him except what he painted.

Except skies, always. He could see those. See them, feel them. His head was in the skies. So the skies in his work are real, consuming. And later, we tramped the cold ether together –

He's at rest, though, now. Fame gave him rest. He no longer haunts this world, homeless. We used to pass each other in the young ones' studios, envy burning us up, a blue flame.

Now he's released, and I must press onwards.

So I come to the very last room.

And I reel back, stunned, thrown backwards so fast I am almost rejoined to my long-lost body. I did not know I could feel such pain. For there she is, my love, my queen, as warm and real as the day I last kissed her, framed in cream fur, black-eyed, wine-lipped. My masterwork, my supreme portrait.

I creep towards her to lie at her feet, almost feeling my dead heart beating.

Under my treasure, there is a label. I start to read their barbarous language. I read it backwards, I read it forwards, and slowly I start to understand, and I laugh with rage, I hack, I cackle.

'Though this remarkable portrait does not share stylistic features with Greco's other works of this period, it is thought to be a portrait of his mistress, Dona Jeronima de las Cuevas, mother of his only child ... the balance of opinion is that no other artist of the period would have been capable of such technical excellence. Note in particular the texture of the fur ...'

But ghost tears blind me, I will read no more.

Curse the bastards who steal my painting! Only one must survive of all of us, one genius, one golden Greco, and everything must bear his name, El Greco must outreach us all. I am scratching, tearing at the stupid label, but I have no hands, I have no nails, I shout with rage but nothing echoes, I am helpless, powerless, once again I fail.

Morning. I have been in a swoon. Servants in livery come to

clean, dull-faced, pushing great whining engines. They trundle through me, gaping like cattle, their eyes never raised to the marvel above.

By daylight she is more glorious than ever. Surely the best thing in all these grand rooms. The young sun glances across my canvas, pauses and pleasures her cheeks, her small nose, the hint of that smile she showed only to me, for with me she was happy, only with me. She told me so, and she could not lie. To me, to me she could not lie. We were friends from childhood, I knew her utterly.

I press my lips against her white narrow hand, leaving no mark, feeling no warmth. Yet the image retains its old teasing beauty, the thrill of the words about to be spoken, the cloak of fur that will soon be laid down ...

But she speaks, she speaks. I listen, amazed. Her slight warm voice across hundreds of years.

'Do not despair. Remember Jorge.'

And it's true, it's true. We were always sure.

And again she whispers, 'My only son. Your Jorge was my only son.'

He had my eyes, and my love of building, my fascination with cunning engines ... He became an architect, and had nine children.

'*Greco fecit.*'

Fool, it was I! My ebony-ivory love and I!

And as she reminds me, I am released.

What's in a name? What's under a name?

In the lee of the Greek are my son and my picture. Her only child, our only child ... The Greek never guessed he had raised a bastard. And so our blood flows on down the ages. And my beautiful portrait is not lost, just borrowed.

In the end, does it matter, since she is saved?

No one can have her as I once had her.

I start to yawn. How odd, I am tired, and it's only nine on this sunny morning. I almost feel I could sleep at last. That patch of true azure in the gallery window. I've had enough. It is time to go home. Those wild white clouds, their flanks of silver, clear air showing through the oil-black *disegno* ...

A blessed blankness beyond the blue.

Thus I surpass him. Time to let go.